Harlequin, the world's No. 1 best-selling publisher of romance fiction, is proud of its tradition of bringing to women everywhere its beautiful and appealing love stories...

Harlequin Romances—warm and wholesome novels that take you to exciting faraway places and reveal the delights of true love.

Harlequin Presents—sophisticated and modern love stories that offer the thrill of exotic locales, and the passions and conflicts of love.

Superromance—longer, exciting, sensual and dramatic new novels, truly contemporary stories in keeping with today's life-styles.

What readers say about Harlequin romance fiction...

"Harlequin books are the doorway to pleasure."

E.W. Hawthorne, California

"They are quality books—down-to-earth reading! Don't ever quit!"

G.F. Buffalo, Minnesota

"A pleasant escape from the pressures of this world."

C.T. Hickory, North Carolina

"Keep them coming! They are still the best books."

R.W., Jersey City, New Jersey

The Mouth of Truth

by

ISOBEL CHACE

Harlequin Books

TORONTO • LONDON • LOS ANGELES • AMSTERDAM
SYDNEY • HAMBURG • PARIS • STOCKHOLM • ATHENS • TOKYO

Original hardcover edition published in 1977
by Mills & Boon Limited

ISBN 0-373-02114-3

Harlequin edition published November 1977

Second printing June 1981

CHAPTER ONE

THE stranger who was also her father looked disapprovingly at her across the huge double desk.

'Your mother tells me you are going to Rome,' he said at last.

Deborah nodded. It was so long since she had seen him that she was fascinated to try and find some familiar ground between them. Looking at his strong, essentially cold features, she could find none. He didn't feel like her father at all.

'With friends?' he prompted her.

'Of course with friends!' she responded immediately. 'You didn't suppose I was going on my own, did you? There's a whole crowd of us going.'

'Hmm. It's not the place I'd choose for you at the moment. We have large business interests in Italy——'

'Have you?' She was only marginally interested. 'But what has that got to do with me?'

'As my daughter——'

Deborah shrugged. 'Do you really think of me like that?' she demanded, knowing the answer with a depressing certainty even before she voiced the question.

'Of course,' he murmured. His face took on a shine of embarrassment. 'I may not have seen much of you in past years, Deborah, but that was not of my choosing. You bear my name, after all, and who else do you suppose has paid your bills all these years?'

Yes, they shared a name, but there had to be more than that, she thought. Was there nothing else between them but a name and a few bills marked paid with thanks?

'I wish we knew each other better,' she said aloud.

'Quite. Perhaps this holiday of yours is the moment for doing so. Why don't you come and stay at our house for a while? Agnes would be pleased to put on some parties for you with people of your own age. You wouldn't be dull with us!'

It was her turn to feel awkward. 'I'd rather not,' she said honestly. She had only met Agnes once, but she had no wish to repeat the experience. 'What have you got against Rome?'

Her father leaned back in his chair. 'Sometimes I think your mother has never got over a childish desire to upset me! I suppose it was she who put this idea into your head?'

'Mother? I don't think so. All she said was that you wouldn't like it and that I'd better talk it over with you myself, because she wasn't going to do your dirty work for you yet again. So what's wrong with Rome?'

Her father sighed. 'The company has been having a lot of bad publicity in Italy these last few weeks, if you must know. I don't like the thought of your being there on your own——'

'But I won't *be* on my own! I'll be with friends!'

'Beside the point, my dear. There won't be anyone there who knows who you are to protect you.'

'*Protect* me? Whatever from?'

Her father looked grim. 'From the enemies of the company. You're not paying attention, Debbie! I've already told you we have large business interests in Italy.'

6

'But they're nothing to do with me!' she said. 'Are they?'

'You're my daughter.'

'Yes, but hardly.' She hoped he wouldn't think she was trying to be rude to him, but he must know that he scarcely felt like a father to her at all. 'None of my friends connect me with you,' she added.

'Don't they know you as Deborah Beaumont?'

'Well, yes, of course they do! But there are hundreds of Beaumonts, after all, and I don't go round boasting that my father is Beaumont's International. Why should I?'

Her father was silent for a long moment. 'You should be proud of Beaumont's,' he said at last. 'It's my life's achievement.'

But one didn't feel proud of something one knew nothing about. However, she recognised the hopelessness of explaining that, or anything like it, to him, and settled instead for a vivid description of the kind of holiday she had in mind.

'It's got nothing to do with business,' she said gently, trying hard not to offend him further. 'And certainly it's got nothing to do with Beaumont's. I'm going to Rome with five friends of mine, none of whom have any money at all, living in the cheapest lodgings we can find—you know the sort of thing. You wouldn't consider it a holiday at all!'

'Probably not.' Her father managed a tired smile. 'And do you intend to wear the kind of garments you have on now? You'll never get into the Vatican dressed like that!'

Deborah looked down at her jeans and sweater with a little frown. 'I'll be taking a dress with me too. I'd have put one on today to come and see you, but your

7

summons rather took me by surprise. You've never insisted on my visiting you here before, have you? I wish you'd tell me what you're afraid might happen to me in Rome instead of muttering about Beaumont's. It must be more than that you don't think my clothes do credit to the firm?'

'My dear Deborah, I'm not totally out of touch with what young people think and wear these days——'

Belatedly, Deborah remembered that he had other children and that though they had Agnes for a mother, an ex-model who had never been seen by anyone including, she suspected, her husband, with a single hair out of place, they probably also wore jeans on occasion.

'No, of course not!' she agreed dutifully.

'Beaumont's has had a very bad time in the Italian Press recently. One would think we'd been infiltrated by the CIA at least, and even the most ordinary business methods have suddenly become suspect. There was a small incident where we were accused of helping a certain politician into power——'

'And did you?'

Mr Beaumont winced. 'I hope not, but it seems likely that we did. It was a good opportunity for getting several contracts for the company—but these things are better done with a certain panache or not at all. If you bungle a thing like that you're asking for trouble!'

'And you got it?'

'We got a great deal of adverse publicity, but we could have weathered that easily enough. No, the worst part of it all was an inquiry into our finances—our *personal* finances, you understand, and certain people in the firm were found to be much better off than anyone had supposed.'

'Including the tax office?' she suggested with only a touch of malice.

'In Italy everyone is in arrears with their taxes. Most people refuse to pay them at all! At least we don't do that!'

Deborah laughed. 'Are you much richer than we all thought?'

Her father did not share her amusement. 'I have no intention of discussing my finances with you, young lady! All I'm saying is that you might be recognised as my daughter while you are in Italy and the results could be extremely harassing for both of us. Won't you change your mind and stay at home this year, Deborah?'

Deborah rose to her feet, feeling a little sorry for the tight-lipped man on the other side of the desk.

'I'm sorry, Father. I want to go and I'm going, but don't worry about it. If anything happens to me, I'll deny any connection between us with my dying breath, so there won't be any comeback on you. Okay?'

'I don't believe you've thought this thing through properly——'

'Probably not,' Deborah agreed gently. 'I'm sorry, Father, but I really can't take it very seriously. All I want to do is have a look at Rome with my friends. Is that really going to bring ruin on your life's work?'

'Let's hope not,' he grunted. 'I'll have to let them know you're coming, that's all. They'll have to deal with it at their end!'

Deborah chewed on the inside of her lip. 'Father, I don't want to be bothered with Beaumont's while I'm away. Can't you understand that it doesn't mean anything to me? It isn't *my* life's work!'

'You're my daughter. Beaumont's may not mean anything to you, but they paid for your schooling——'

'So what, Father?'

'You owe me and the firm some gratitude for that, surely?'

Deborah stared at him. 'Do you grudge what I cost you?' she demanded, now as angry as he.

'Of course not, but I am your father and I think you should listen to my advice, especially when I'm only thinking of your own good.'

'Are you?' Her mother would have recognised the light of battle in her sea-green eyes at once, but her father was less observant and knew her less well. 'Aren't you thinking of the firm?'

'It's the same thing, my dear,' he protested. 'Beaumont's supports us all—your mother as well as yourself, I may point out!'

'My mother is supported by you, I agree,' she said slowly and clearly, 'but I am not. You bought Agnes, and maybe you can buy your other children, but you won't buy me! Goodbye, Father. I'll send you a card from Rome!'

'*Deborah!*'

She had, she supposed, been unpardonably rude, but she didn't care. She walked out the door, slamming it behind her, nodding to her father's surprised secretary as she went. She was burning with rage, and with humiliation too. What kind of person did he think she was? Some puppet who could be controlled by pulling the strings like he did with everyone else? Well, she was not! And if she had to go to Rome to prove her point to him once and for all, then to Rome she would go!

The plane was completely full as most charter flights are. Not for the first time, Deborah wished that her friends could have had their luggage pared down to a ruthless minimum by her mother as had happened to her. Even though Michael Doyle had insisted she should take the window-seat, he had then proceeded to load her up with packages, his friendly, sheepish grin effectively destroying any protest she might have made.

'Only the rich have suitcases to be stowed neatly away in the luggage hold,' he said. 'You shouldn't mix with the idle poor and then these little inconveniences wouldn't happen to you.'

Deborah was used to being teased about her riches. Once or twice she had explained that they were her mother's riches rather than hers and that she was no richer than anyone else, but she had to admit that most of her friends weren't even rich by association and, she supposed, if the worst ever came to the worst, she had the comfortable knowledge that she would be rescued from her plight while they had no such assurance. Michael certainly hadn't. She had never even heard that he had any relatives. He was always on his own and would be now if she had not come along and taken him in tow. He was the cleverest person she knew. His intelligence shone out of his thin, bony face and knotted his digestion whenever she relaxed her vigilance over his diet, which wasn't often these days because she, who had never suffered a twinge of indigestion in her life, found his patient suffering in the face of chronic heartburn more than she could bear.

Michael made stained-glass windows for a hobby. He had sold some recently and it was that which had enabled him to come to Rome.

'I want to study the churches,' he had said.

'The stained glass too?' she had asked him.

He had shaken his head. 'Not their tradition, thanks be to God. They distract me from all the other things

11

I want to see in France, where it's their tradition. I hope I don't see a single coloured window in the whole of Rome!'

Deborah didn't much mind either way. 'I'm glad we're going together,' she had said, and she had kissed him with rather more enthusiasm than she had actually felt because somehow everybody always paired her off with Michael and, if he was the best and most romantic thing in her life, she thought she should do something to encourage him.

Her other friends who made up their particular party had paired off long before she and Michael had come on the scene. John and Mary were both nice and blessedly unexciting. Patty had a kittenish prettiness and was quite the most selfish person Deborah had ever known and, therefore, perhaps it was only just that Jerry, dark, moody, and motivated by a spiteful envy of anyone better off than himself, should have caught her attention, for if anyone could stand up to her exclusive interest in herself and her own affairs it was he.

As the plane rose into the cloudy skies, Deborah wondered for the first time if she had been wise to come. She went back over her interview with her father and wished she had waited long enough to find out what was at the bottom of his wanting to keep her at home. She should be used to his summing up people and relationships in terms of money by now. Her mother, who had suffered from it much more than Deborah ever would, was far more tolerant of her erstwhile husband.

'He can't help it, love. Don't expect more from him than he has to give. That was my mistake. I couldn't see the high price he put on me as a compliment, but there are people who do see it that way, and good luck to them!'

12

People like Agnes, for instance! Deborah had once seen her wheedle a fur coat out of her father and had felt nothing more than contempt for her. She had never pretended to her mother's easy tolerance of others' limitations. She was young enough to have no wish to compromise with the ideals that burned within her and, if others should fall by the wayside, she saw that as no excuse for herself—*she* was her own woman and she wouldn't crawl to anyone, not even her highly numerate father!

And this time he had to be joking! She was indistinguishable from her friends, dressed as she was in the uniform they all adopted of jeans and windcheaters, chunky, unisex jewellery, and hair that flopped about her shoulders and got in her eyes almost all the time. Good heavens, her own mother sometimes couldn't pick her out from the crowd, so how should anyone else be able to?

In that she was being less than honest with herself. Her hair was so fair as to be almost silver; and she was graced with a perfect complexion; pretty, neat features; and eyes that held a touch of mystery like the deep recesses of the sea. Once seen she was seldom forgotten and, in a place like Rome, her colouring if nothing else was bound to make her startling even to the casual observer.

She turned impulsively towards Michael. 'You won't go off by yourself without me, will you?' she pleaded with him. 'I don't mind at home, but I don't fancy being on my own in Rome.'

He grinned at her. 'Don't you like having your bottom pinched?'

That hadn't occurred to her. 'No, I don't,' she admitted, 'but it isn't that——'

'So you do like it!' He made to attack her with an importunate finger and thumb, earning a sharp slap from her.

'Don't! That isn't what I was talking about! I just don't want to be alone in a strange city. I'm hopeless at finding my way about, if you must know!'

He laughed out loud. 'Oh, come on, Debbie! Who guides me on and off the London buses when I'm all set to go off in the opposite direction to the one I want to go?'

'But I know London! I don't know Rome.'

He cast her a thoughtful glance. 'Is something else worrying you? You came back from visiting your father looking grim, but I didn't think anything of it. Was it bad news?'

'I don't know. He didn't want me to come, and that annoyed me a bit. He didn't say why not, and then I lost my temper as I always do when we're together for longer than ten minutes put together. Mama says we're too alike, but I hope she's wrong. I'd hate to have his outlook on life!'

'Or have to live with the delectable Agnes!' Michael agreed with feeling. 'How d'you know she wasn't at the back of spoiling your holiday for you? It would be just like her, grudging every penny your old man gives to anyone else!'

Deborah looked at him in horror. 'You don't suppose my father *paid* for me to come, do you? I earned every penny myself! Why, I wouldn't touch his money with a barge-pole!'

'Wouldn't you? You may have to one day.'

Deborah was shocked. 'But I wouldn't!'

'You would if it were for your own family,' he told her stoutly. 'Imagine yourself as married with any num-

14

ber of children and your husband longing to do his own thing rather than make money for you all. You'd ask him soon enough then.'

'No, I wouldn't. I'd starve first.'

'Well, your husband wouldn't!' Michael maintained. 'At least, I wouldn't! With all that lovely money lying about, I'd make sure I got my hands on it one way or another.'

Deborah raised her eyebrows. 'Then it's a good thing you're not going to be my husband, isn't it?' she said as lightly as she could. 'Because I would never permit such a thing!'

'I could persuade you—you know I could!' Michael grinned.

Deborah moved a couple of inches away from him. 'No, you couldn't. Don't flatter yourself, Michael Doyle! I like you, but there are quite a lot of things I wouldn't do for you—and that's one of them!'

Michael shifted more comfortably in his seat. 'We'll see! One of these days we'll see if you don't, my love! I'm the biggest thing in your life and you know it.'

Deborah was silent. It was sad to think the horizons of her life were as limited as he suggested, but up to now it was probably true. Perhaps Rome would bring something new, only with Michael by her side she was beginning to doubt it. She felt as though she had never really seen Michael before, and she didn't much like what she saw now. The truth came to her like a blazing flash from heaven. Michael Doyle bored her! He was nice and she liked him out of habit, but he bored her silly! She knew exactly what he was going to do at least two seconds before he knew it himself and for months now she had secretly resented the way he fiddled with

15

his money in his wallet and pocket as if it hurt him physically to part with any of it.

She could only sigh with relief when they started to lose height, preparatory to landing at Rome Airport, called after Leonardo da Vinci. The tyres screeched against the ground and bounced uncomfortably as the engines were pushed into reverse thrust to brake the plane.

'Not the best landing ever!' Michael remarked.

Deborah wasn't experienced enough to judge. She undid her seat-belt with a rising sense of excitement and tried to push Michael's parcels back into his arms before she got landed with carrying them off the plane. He accepted them with such obvious reluctance that she was amused and made no comment when he pushed his way out ahead of her, jumping into the bus as fast as he could in order to acquire a seat where he could spread his possessions all round him.

They had a long wait for their luggage to come into the terminal building. In the face of the sharp elbows of the other passengers jostling for position by the moving belt where it was expected, the six of them knotted into a defensive group intent on keeping their place. That was, all of them except Deborah, who had a thing about people pressing against her and would willingly have left her suitcase going slowly round and round until every last piece had been collected sooner than have to fight for it in the general mêlée.

'Are you expecting me to get your suitcase for you with all these things in my hands?' Michael demanded, exasperated by her craven attitude.

'I'm not expecting you to get it at all,' she returned calmly. 'What's the hurry?'

This was too much for Michael. 'We have to catch

the bus into Rome! We're in a *hurry*!'

'I'm not. Okay, so we miss the first bus, there's bound to be another one.'

'But when? Debbie, do hurry yourself! You know I can't stand waiting around!'

Deborah allowed herself to be hung about once more with his possessions and watched with a suppressed shudder as he forced his way between two middle-aged women, knocking them sideways as he went, and emerged triumphant with her suitcase in his hand.

'It's heavy,' he told her. 'Look, you carry on with my stuff and I'll carry yours. Okay?'

Deborah didn't think much of the arrangement, particularly when she saw her suitcase being put into the luggage compartment of the bus by the driver. That was another thing that annoyed her about Michael. He was so pleased with himself when he thought he had got the better of someone else. He was pleased with himself now as his jaunty step bore witness. It was irresistible not to want to wipe the smile off his face.

'You have to buy the tickets inside,' she said. 'It says so on the notice. Eight hundred lire per passenger. Shall I give you mine now?'

'No.' His eyes didn't quite meet hers. 'I'll pay for you.'

'Why?'

He glared at her. 'Well, hang it all, Debbie, it's expected that the man should pay every now and then for his girl-friend. It makes him feel good.'

It was not Deborah's experience that parting with money ever made Michael feel good, but she didn't want to spoil his big moment for him.

'Thanks very much. I'll enjoy it twice as much as a gift from you.'

He smiled. 'That's the spirit! You're far too independent for a girl, my love!'

Deborah, still carrying his strange assortment of packages, climbed on to the bus and settled herself on a seat towards the rear. She made a pile of most of the bags on her knee, putting a stray and rather torn envelope into the pocket of her jacket in case it got lost. The others crowded round her, eager for their first sight of the Eternal City.

'Where's Michael?' they asked her.

'Getting the tickets.'

Mary, who was far more acute than she looked, winked deliberately at Deborah. 'For all of us?' she mocked.

'Good heavens, no!' Deborah answered.

'Perhaps he's lost himself. Would it be a terrible loss to you?'

'No,' said Deborah.

'If you're wise, you'll tell him that before you're much older,' Mary advised. 'He's far too fond of money ever to let you go easily.'

'But I haven't any money!' Deborah said.

'You don't have to pretend with us, Debbie. We all know who your father is, and that you've never been short of a penny in your whole life! We admire you for not ramming it down our throats, but don't kid yourself that you've ever deceived Michael! He wouldn't pass the time of day with you if you were as poor as we are!'

Patty stopped admiring herself in the mirror of her flapjack and turned her face towards the other two girls. 'You worry too much, Mary. If I were Deborah, I'd admire Michael for trying to insure his future properly.

18

That lad's going far, and he'll take his wife with him. What more can anyone ask?'

'Is that all you ask of Jerry?' Mary drawled.

Patty looked smug. 'Jerry and I will make out,' she claimed.

Nobody doubted it, though Mary was far too nice to say so. Deborah saw the quiet exchange between her and John as he came on to the bus and felt a sharp pang of jealousy at their obvious contentment in each other. What was the matter with her, she wondered, that nobody seemed to want her for herself? She would have to make it quite clear that her father's money was nothing to do with her and she didn't think Michael would linger long in her company after that. It was bound to leave a gap in her life, but although she couldn't quite believe it, she was beginning to think it would be a nice miss not to have him around.

He hurried on to the bus just as it was pulling out of the terminal. There was a short delay as it went round to another building where the national flights came in and they picked up another couple of passengers. Then, almost immediately, they were on the road for Rome, rushing through the countryside and the coral pink blocks of flats that made up the most modern and least attractive of the suburbs.

Rome itself came as a surprise. Suddenly the Colosseum was before them, the upper floors caved in and sadly pockmarked where the bronze pins had been removed by later builders too idle to quarry and shape their own marble. Only on one side did the amphitheatre still retain its original height, but even so, it was hard to imagine how it had looked when covered with white and gleaming marble and with a statue looking outwards from each of the upper arches.

19

It was not long after that that they arrived at the main railway station. Everyone piled out into the roadway, dodging the oncoming traffic as best they could. Deborah made a dash for the pavement, leaving Michael to retrieve her suitcase. She placed his collection of paper bags between her feet, leaving her hands free to search in her handbag for the address of the apartment where they were to stay.

'Miss Beaumont?'

She looked up quickly, marginally surprised to be accosted by the smartly dressed chauffeur who addressed her. Her father again!

'How did you know?' she asked him.

He pointed across to Michael. 'I asked your friends. You, Miss Beaumont, are to come with me. I have instructions——'

'Oh no!' she exclaimed. 'I'm staying with my friends! Tell my father that, will you? And while you're about it, tell him to leave me alone!'

The chauffeur looked almost sorry for her. 'I'm sorry, Miss Beaumont, I have my instructions to collect you and deliver you to the Palazzo Manzù. No doubt you will have every opportunity to voice your objections to the Signor Manzù himself. Please step into the car?'

Deborah braced her feet against the pavement. '*Michael!*' she yelled.

Michael came reluctantly over to her. 'Don't shout, Debbie! Can't you see everyone is looking at you!'

Deborah drew herself up to her full height. 'Michael, this man has been sent to fetch me by my father's *friends*. Will you please tell him that I'm staying where I am!'

'But, Debbie——'

She sighed, exasperated by his spinelessness. 'But what?'

'Don't you think you ought to go with him? What good will it do to antagonise your old man? You can always come back to us as soon as you've got everything sorted out. You've got the address where we're staying, haven't you?'

'I suppose so.' She cast a rebellious look in his direction. 'Don't you understand? I don't want to go!'

Silently he held out her suitcase to her, but she refused to take it. 'Whatever happens, I won't need that!' she declared. She hesitated. 'Michael, don't make me go!'

'But if your father——'

She bit her lip. 'Supposing it isn't my father? Supposing it has nothing to do with him?'

Some emotion she couldn't put a name to flickered for an instant in Michael's eyes. 'It has to be your father,' he said.

CHAPTER TWO

DEBORAH had no idea where the car was taking her.

'Who is this Signor Manzù?' she asked the chauffeur.

'You will soon see, *signorina*. He had to be at a meeting or he would have met you himself. My orders were to meet you and then to pick him up. Ah, there he is now!'

He pointed out a man standing on the edge of the

pavement, a man well over six feet in height and with powerful shoulders that seemed the more so because of the slimness of his hips and the length of his legs. His clothes fitted him as though they had been specially made for him and, as the car drew in beside where he was standing, she thought it likely they had been, for the material was as superb as their cut. But it was his expression that dominated her attention. He looked both arrogant and angry and, in some way she couldn't define, she was more than a little afraid of him.

He got in beside her in a single, lithe movement. His eyes travelled over her without curiosity.

'You came, I see, Miss Beaumont,' he remarked.

'Under protest!'

His eyebrows shot upwards. 'Most people do not come to stay at the Manzù home under protest——'

'I suppose,' she cut him off, 'you are a friend of my father's?'

He shrugged his shoulders. 'No, Miss Beaumont, I am not. I have never had the pleasure of meeting your father. In fact you are the first member of his family to cross my path. But not the last, I hope,' he added, with such studied politeness she could have mistaken it for insolence.

'Then why kidnap me?' she demanded.

'Kidnap?' To her indignation he was amused. 'I suppose you could call it that,' he admitted. 'I imagine your father would pay a handsome reward for you?'

'For me? I doubt it. If you wanted to make your fortune, you should have captured my stepmother, Agnes,' she told him.

'But your stepmother wasn't fool enough to come to Rome on her own,' he retorted smoothly. 'You'd better give up and come quietly, Miss Beaumont.'

'Never! I'll never forgive my father for this!'

Her captor leaned back in his seat, surveying her through half-closed eyes. 'Let's hope he forgives you. You must be worth more to him than you think or you wouldn't be in your present predicament. I hope you have other clothes with you, incidentally, as those are not suitable for the place where you'll be staying.'

'I have only these!' Deborah took a pride in being able to tell him so. 'What are you going to do about that?'

He favoured her with a slanting smile. 'I'll think of something. I expect your father will think that, at least, cheap at the price!'

Something in his voice made Deborah blink. Had she imagined that touch of menace? Could he really be intending to hold her to ransom?

'What are you going to do with me?' she asked, trying to control her voice.

'For the moment I'm going to take you home with me—and, *signorina*, while you are there as my guest, you will behave yourself and play the part of the charming young lady I have told my family you are. Is it understood?'

'You've made a mistake! I'm staying with my friends——' He shook his head at her and she swallowed the lump that had formed in her throat. 'My father won't pay a penny for *me*!' she added in panic.

'We shall see. He should have warned you not to come to Italy just now, when kidnapping is an everyday occurrence and his firm has just been the subject of very bad publicity. But perhaps he doesn't see much of you?'

'I live with my mother,' she confided. 'He did tell me not to come,' she added, unable to bring herself not to defend her father even in circumstances such as these. 'I didn't believe him!'

'But you believe him now?'

'I haven't much choice, have I?' she said.

His look was not unkind. 'It won't be as bad as you think,' he soothed her. 'When you are ready to see reason and give me your promise not to return to those friends of yours, I'll see to it that you miss nothing in the way of seeing Rome while you're here. If, in the meantime, you find it inconvenient being my guest, you will have only yourself to blame. I shall be as harsh a guard as you force me to be—no more, no less.'

Deborah made an abortive attempt to gain the door-handle and let herself out of the car. His response was immediate. He scooped her up tight against him with an iron arm, immobilising her once and for all.

'You may not think much of your father's money,' he rebuked her, 'but you have all the ill-disciplined attributes of a brat born with a silver spoon in her mouth. Rest easy, sweetheart! You're coming with me whether you like it or not!'

'And who decided that?' she demanded. 'My father, or you?'

'Does it make any difference? You are in my care now, and that means doing as you're told.' His fingers nipped her flesh and she was aware of him as she had never been of another human being. The heat of her cheeks took her breath away and she shut her eyes the better to ignore him. Why should she obey him? And who was he anyway?

'Please let me go,' she said, her voice tinged with ice.

He did so, giving her a last, warning tap on her arm. She sat as far away from him as she could, wedging

24

the arm-rest into the small of her back, while she tried to collect her scattered wits.

'How long do you plan to hold me?' she asked.

His lips twitched. 'I'm not holding you, but I don't mind doing so if you want me to.'

Deborah concentrated with difficulty on the point she was trying to make. 'What happens if my father won't pay you for my safe return?'

He gave her an amused look. 'There's no danger of that! Relax, *signorina*, and enjoy the experience of staying in one of the most famous palaces in Rome. Surely that is not asking too much of you?'

'I prefer to be with my friends!' she retorted. 'With Michael——'

His amusement turned to a thinly veiled contempt. 'Have you known him long?' he inquired.

'A couple of years. He's a very clever artist.'

The man dismissed Michael with a casual shrug. 'What are your particular interests, Miss Beaumont?'

'I sculpt. I do some portraits and a lot of ultra-modern stuff. You wouldn't understand them. Sometimes I don't understand them myself. I draw a bit too, but I prefer the tactile quality of sculpting. I like to feel the shape beneath my fingers.' She glanced down at her shirt and jeans. 'These are my working clothes,' she explained, 'but I did have some others with me. I didn't want to look different from the others.' She came to an abrupt stop, more annoyed with herself than ever. It wasn't any business of this man's what she wore, or if her present garments did bear the marks of weeks of toil. If she had had one tenth of the poise she had thought she had had a few hours before, she wouldn't have cared what she was wearing, and she certainly wouldn't have cared what her captor thought of her appearance.

His eyebrows rose. 'I didn't know you're an artist,' he said.

'That's putting it a bit strong,' she murmured. 'I still think of myself as an art student, but I hope to get over it soon. It takes a while to break out of the chrysalis of needing someone else's approval——'

'And you got that from Michael?'

'I suppose so,' she admitted. 'He doesn't like my work much, which makes it all the better that he can't dismiss it as unimportant. He knows what he's talking about when it comes to art, you see. He's very receptive and not at all prejudiced. He can appreciate most of the greats in a way I don't begin to, and it doesn't matter to him whether it's a work by Michelangelo himself or from a complete unknown. That's worth having.'

The man took her hand in his, exploring her palm with the soft side of his thumb. 'Is that all you need from him?' he asked.

Nettled, Deborah tried to take her hand away from him. 'Of course not!'

'Oh well, you won't be seeing him for a while,' the man said smoothly. 'I'll have to see to it that you don't miss him too much.' He leaned forward a little and smiled directly at her. 'Does your interest in art extend to fashion?'

'Sometimes,' she agreed cautiously.

'Good, then you won't mind seeing what the Corso can produce in the way of a new wardrobe for you.'

Deborah had heard of the Corso as being Rome's equivalent of Bond Street. 'I doubt I can afford to do my shopping there. Couldn't we go somewhere else?'

'Kidnapped persons don't normally expect to pay for

26

such trifles, surely?' he teased her gently. 'It's all part of the plot to have you dress like a lady instead of like— an art student, shall we say? Roman elegance is famous for transforming girls into raving beauties. That should appeal to you at least!'

'I can't accept clothes from someone I don't know,' she said firmly. 'It wouldn't be proper. Why, I don't even accept clothes from my father!'

'Pity, because in a way these clothes will be coming from your father. He'll be footing the bill in the end.'

'You hope,' Deborah put in. 'He'd be a fool to give in to your crazy demands! Why, who knows whom you'll be kidnapping next if you're allowed to get away with it?'

'Your moral indignation is duly noted,' he answered, looking amused. 'But kidnapping is becoming so common in Italy as to be soon quite respectable. It's an easy way of raising money and there is very little risk attached.'

Anyone who looked less in need of money would be hard to find, Deborah reflected. The car was large and obviously expensive, and the man's clothes looked bespoke, and English besides. She didn't believe that he had kidnapped her for money! She wasn't sure he had kidnapped her at all.

'How did your chauffeur know who I was?' she wondered aloud.

'I showed him your photograph and described you a little. I have a good memory for faces, even when only seen in pictures, especially when their owners are female, blonde, and very beautiful!'

She tried to think of where he could have seen a picture of herself, but only succeeded in feeling more muddled than before. Her mother kept her photograph

27

beside her bed and, she supposed, her father had one of her too, but Agnes would have seen to it that it was never publicly displayed. Besides, what could this man possibly have to do with her father?

'I don't even know your name?' she said carefully.

'You may call me Domenico. Domenico Manzù. Are you any wiser?'

'No, but you didn't intend me to be. Is Manzù really your family name?'

'Of course. Why should I lie to you?'

'I don't know. Supposing when I get free of you I report you to the police? If I were to tell them your name it wouldn't take them long to pick you up, would it?'

He laughed. 'When I set you free, *signorina*, the last place you will go is to the police! You will be as well trained as a homing pigeon and will want to come straight back to me!'

Now he was being deliberately rude, she thought. 'Never! Do you suppose I *like* being kidnapped?'

Her indignation had no visible effect on him. 'It will be something for you to look back on when you are an old lady. Think what a romantic adventure it will seem to you then.' He flicked a look over her face and figure which set her heart pounding within her.

'I haven't a romantic disposition,' she said. 'If I had, I'd have treated you to a fine display of hysterics by now!'

'I have coped with hysterics before,' he said dryly. 'If you feel you may succumb, remember I am just as likely to slap you as to kiss you.'

'Either fate would be as bad as the other!' she claimed.

'You think so?' His face remained as hard as ever and

his expression as contemptuous. It was not surprising Deborah was afraid of him.

They travelled in silence for a while. Deborah pushed her hands into the pockets of her jacket, because now that the first excitement of being kidnapped was over, she felt cold inside and she didn't want *him* to know she was shaking like a jelly. A piece of paper met her fingers and she drew it out, thinking it would calm her to read something that had nothing to do with her present predicament. She was surprised to find it was addressed to Michael. She turned the envelope over and was astonished to see the crest of her father's firm clearly embossed on the back. Her mouth went dry. She turned it over and over in her hands, trying to justify her desire to open it up and find out what her father could have had to say to Michael of all people! How on earth had he come to know about him? Yet there was his address and his name, down to his middle initial, neatly typed on the outside.

Her fingers crumpled the envelope as they pulled it apart. Inside was a cheque made out by her father in Michael's favour, and it was for *five hundred pounds*!

'Good heavens!' She hadn't meant to say the words out loud, but she must have done, for Signor Manzù took the cheque from her listless fingers and transferred it to his own pocket.

'Why the surprise? Didn't you realise that there was always a danger that money was the main cause of that young man's interest in you? Your father has good reason to be concerned for you, don't you think?'

Deborah wished she knew. 'He never has been before. Besides, he never would have given Michael such a sum for me! It's quite a lot of money.'

A muscle pulled at the corner of Signor Manzù's

mouth. 'Not very much, but it will help pay for some of your new clothes. You underrate your father, *cara*. He'll pay much more than that for your safety—you'll see!'

She sighed. 'He won't like it. He has Agnes and all his other children to consider——'

'That doesn't make you less his daughter,' he said with a gentleness she had not found in him before. The car slowed to a stop. 'This is no time for sadness! You must smile and look happy, for we are arriving at my home and people will wonder if you continue to look so miserable!'

It was difficult not to be impressed by the fine building before her, despite the peeling paint and the rickety attachments to the shutters. There was a very fine stone staircase that curved upwards on either side to an elaborately carved front door.

'It's magnificent enough to be a palace!' she observed as she went before him up the stone steps, her hand lingering on the crumbling crest that decorated the bottom of the balustrade.

'It is a palace. My family have lived here since the Middle Ages. Parts of the building still date from then, but much of it was rebuilt in Napoleonic times. Come inside, Debbie, and meet my family.'

But Deborah hung back. 'I wish I were wearing something else!' She made a face at her jeans. 'Funny, really, if anyone had asked me I should have said I was ideally dressed for being kidnapped—and then you have to bring me to a place like this! Whoever heard of anyone wearing jeans in a palace?'

He was amused. 'I'm afraid you'll have to wait until we've bought you something more suitable. Cheer up, little one, I will tell them you are a sculptor and that will explain everything!'

30

Deborah told herself that a kidnap victim—if that was what she was, and she still had her doubts about that—was not expected to be a social success, and certainly not to be nervous about whether the captor's family should like her or not, but, all the same, she could not resist peering at herself in the large, speckled glass on the wall in the hall and tried to smooth down her tangled, knotted hair. She might have made an effort to renew her make-up as well, but something in the way Domenico Manzù was looking at her brought the colour rushing into her face. It was a very masculine look, against which her present clothing was a most inadequate defence.

'Ready?' he asked her. He held out his hands for her jacket, but she shook her head, pulling her shirt forward over her breasts with fretful fingers. The movement amused him and she cursed herself for being so obvious.

'How many are there in your family?' she asked him, recovering a little of her usual poise.

'At the moment only my mother and my sister are staying here, but I have two brothers also. They need not concern you for the moment, however. My sister's fiancé calls frequently, but as yet he does not live here.'

So, she thought, he didn't much care for his prospective brother-in-law. She hoped the dislike was mutual, for an ally in the household who came and went at will was bound to be useful.

'And do they all know that you've kidnapped me?' she pressed him.

'They will not believe you if you tell them so,' he responded dryly. 'As far as they are concerned you are the daughter of a business acquaintance come to stay with us.'

She was immediately indignant. 'You expect me to pretend to such a thing when you've brought me here against my will?'

He put his hand on her shoulder and smiled at her. 'You won't find it half as difficult as you think. They haven't the least reason for disliking you, you know. They will be delighted to have such a pretty guest to stay with them!'

'Even an involuntary guest?' Strangely, she didn't sound either cross or frightened, but only eager for a new experience that might never have come her way otherwise. How many people did one know who had actually stayed in a Roman palace? Deborah didn't know any. More, she had never before met anybody who had pretensions to being a member of the Black Nobility who, less now than before, had made up the secular court of the Pope. Nowadays the papacy was trying to shed most of the trappings of monarchy and the Black Nobility were no longer as important as in former times, but there was still an aura about the old names, Catholic and respectable to a man, and to the ancient offices that many of them still held within the Vatican, the small area to which the Pope's former possessions have been reduced. Who knew, Deborah said to herself, the famous people, perhaps even the Popes themselves, who had preceded her as guests within these noble portals? That was a thrill enough for anyone!

Domenico Manzù's lips twitched. 'I see you are becoming resigned to your fate at last. If you will allow yourself to be, you will be very happy here as our guest, no?'

He bent his head towards her and smiled. Deborah took fright and withdrew hastily into herself. She had the unpleasing notion that he had meant to kiss her and the idea that he should do so was somehow shocking to her.

'Please don't!'

'You object to such an innocent salute?' he questioned her.

'Yes, I think I do,' she said.

The look he gave her was intimate and therefore unwelcome to her. His eyes mocked her indignant glance. 'Only think? Shall I change your mind for you?'

'Certainly not!' she said with resolution. Her eyes fell before his. 'It isn't fair to take advantage of me when I'm supposed to be your guest. It isn't fair!' she added in harassed tones, thus completely ruining her effect.

'You have a ready tongue with which to defend yourself, however,' he murmured.

Her eyes flashed. 'I am still your prisoner!'

His amusement disconcerted her. 'Remember that,' he warned her, 'before you tempt me to forget your reluctance to be here. I should find it very easy to forget,' he added with an irony that made the back of her neck prickle.

'I'm scarcely likely to forget it!' she retorted tartly. 'But if you so much as lay a finger on me, I'll scream the house down! What would your family think then, *signore*?'

His casual shrug made her temper flare within her. 'That I am a man and easily tempted,' he answered her. 'What else should they think?'

'I'm sure they'd be very shocked if they saw you kissing me against my will. Why, my mother would blow a fuse if she were to find *me*——'

He pushed her hair back behind her ears. 'That is one of the advantages of being a man, *signorina*. My family, like yours, would undoubtedly be far more

33

shocked at your allowing me to kiss you than by my doing so. It's the way of the world!'

She opened her eyes wide. 'You mean they'd blame *me*?'

He considered her in silence for a moment. 'I am sure you would consider that to be unfair also,' he commented at last, 'but they would undoubtedly do so. Shall we go in now so that you can meet them?'

She nodded, wishing she had the power to devastate his arrogant confidence in himself with a few well chosen words. She cast a last, brief look at herself in the glass and caught a glimpse of someone who shared her features but whom she didn't know at all. This stranger was far from looking the reluctant, misused captive of her imagination. On the contrary, there was a distinct sparkle in her eyes that spoke volumes about the anticipation with which she looked forward to seeing more of the Manzù palace and the treasures it contained. Her spirits were obviously, nay blatantly, uncrushed by the adventure in which she was an unwilling participant.

The drawing room was large by any standards. The huge expanse of marble floor was covered here and there by expensive rugs, and groups of exquisite French furniture huddled together for support at intervals with a lack of cosiness that made Deborah wonder why the Manzùs didn't close the room and meet elsewhere. But apparently she was alone in feeling overwhelmed by such surroundings. Domenico's mother, dressed in the inevitable black of Mediterranean widowhood, was seated on one of the fragile gilded chairs at the far end of the room, the cane in her hand resting on the floor between her immaculately shod feet. She watched her son's approach through half-closed eyes, seeming not to see Deborah at all.

'You are late,' she greeted her son.

'But in a good cause,' he returned with a faint smile. 'We have a guest from England, Mamma. Unhappily, her luggage has been mislaid, so she asks you to excuse her choice of dress for luncheon.' He led Deborah forward by the hand, his fingers as hard as steel against her wrist as she momentarily hung back. 'Miss Deborah Beaumont, Mamma. Debbie, my mother, the Signora Manzù.'

Deborah extended her hand. 'How do you do?'

The Signora inclined her head graciously. 'Do you speak any Italian, Miss Beaumont? Not that it matters in this household, but my daughter's fiancé is not a linguist.'

'I'm afraid I don't,' Deborah admitted. 'I tried to learn a few words before I came, but until you hear people actually speaking all around you, it's hard to believe in it as a serious proposition.'

'I understand exactly,' the older woman acknowledged. 'I used to feel like that about German. Surely, I would tell myself, they don't actually speak this language to each other. We were soon to discover that they did! But you are too young to know anything about those days! What are you doing in Italy?'

Deborah opened her mouth to reply but was as speedily cut off by Signor Manzù. 'She sculpts, Mamma, and came with a group of other young artists to see Rome. Her father is Beaumont International, though, and he preferred she should stay with us *en famille* in view of all the kidnappings there have been recently in Rome and the bad press his company has been having.'

Deborah stared at him, not knowing whether to believe him or not. If it were not true, it was certainly an audacious lie! 'Beaumont International is nothing to do with me!' she declared.

The Signora Manzù's eyes snapped with amusement. 'You would sooner be with your friends?' she suggested. 'How young people have changed from my day! In your place I should have found it irresistible to have Domenico constantly at my side to protect me from these bad men!'

Deborah's smile reached her eyes, bringing out the green glints in her irises. 'I'm sorry to say I don't trust your son, *signora*. I think he may be a wolf in sheep's clothing.'

It took a second for the older woman to understand the illusion, then she shrugged. 'Who wants to be at the mercy of a silly sheep, *cara*? But you are wise to be careful! My friends tell me that Domenico is seldom to be seen with the same girl twice! You must see to it that he looks after you properly while you are in Rome. It is more than time that some nice girl took him in hand and put an end to his flitting from one flower to the next. I shall rely on you to encourage him to take stock of his responsibilities for the future. Will you do this for me?'

'I'll do my best, *signora*,' Deborah smiled. She eyed Domenico from beneath her lashes to see how he was taking his mother's teasing and quailed at the look in his eyes. Apparently she had made his mother the wrong answer. 'I shall want to see my own friends too,' she added on a pugnacious note. 'Especially Michael!'

'While you are in Rome and are my guest I shall naturally do all I can to entertain you,' he promised gracefully, bowing over her hand. 'If I am noble enough to take you shopping this afternoon, I shall expect to

36

have your exclusive attention for the rest of the day. Is that fair, *signorina*?'

'This afternoon, yes, but don't expect me to ignore my friends all the time I'm here, because I won't!'

'Your father would prefer it if you did,' he answered dryly, 'but I'm prepared to settle for your company only for the time when I can look after you personally. Is that a deal?'

He held out his hand to her and she had put her own in his before she had time to change her mind.

'I suppose you think I've given you my word now, but I can't promise not to try to reach my friends. I came to Rome in the first place to be with them.'

'If I were you I would choose my friends more carefully,' he responded, looking grim. 'And I do think you have given your word, *signorina*. I am looking forward to being proved right to trust in a woman's honour. You will not disappoint me?'

'Domenico!' his mother protested. 'If these are friends of Miss Beaumont's——'

'Friends! Deborah's father is a rich man, Mamma, a fact which Deborah may ignore but which her friends do not! She is being ridiculous when she shows such loyalty to those she would be far better off without! One cannot help but question their motives——'

The Signora looked upset. 'I think this cannot be any business of yours, my son,' she said quickly, her concern written clearly on her face. 'If Miss Beaumont likes them, why should she doubt that they like her too? And if they sometimes accept her father's largesse, what is that to do with you?'

Deborah's mouth twisted into a wry smile. 'Most people sit up and take notice when money is concerned, don't they, *signore*?'

Domenico gave her a fiery look. 'If that is your experience, who am I to gainsay you? However, I think you will admit that here you have every comfort, which is more than these friends of yours would have provided you with!'

'Why shouldn't I admit it? That doesn't mean I shouldn't prefer my friends' poverty to——'

'Careful, *cara*,' he warned her. 'This afternoon I shall put these claims of yours to the test. It won't be my fault if the Mouth of Truth nips your fingers off!' His expression relaxed into a smile. 'Have you heard of our Mouth of Truth, *signorina*?'

She shook her head. She would have liked to have questioned him about it, but at that moment a maid came into the room and announced that lunch was ready and waiting for them in the dining room. Signora Manzù gathered them up and led the way firmly from one enormous room to another, protesting that her hunger would brook no further delays, not even for Deborah to examine the many works of art that decorated the dining room.

'Food,' she declared, 'is the greatest art of them all! And the only one that can't be put off until tomorrow for one's full attention. A good meal waits for no man! Some good pasta and a fine wine is all one needs to make the world seem a different place! Don't you agree, my dear?'

And, not a little amused by such a forthright declaration of the proper priorities in life, Deborah admitted that she did.

CHAPTER THREE

FROM her bedroom window Deborah could see some of the umbrella pines for which Rome is famous. Their scent came up into the room, beckoning her to the freedom she would find outside the Manzù palace if only she could find some way to escape. Yet there were many attractions inside her comfortable prison too. She admitted the fact to herself reluctantly, ashamed by her own spinelessness in not really wanting to escape—not until she had seen the marvellous works of art that she knew the palace contained! Any artist would want to do that, she comforted herself, so why not she?

Domenico Manzù tapped on her open door. 'How do you find my palace?' he asked her.

'Lush,' she said. Offhand, it was the most horrible thing she could think of to say. 'Too lush for everyday living,' she added.

He glanced round the room. 'Even in here?'

Her eyes followed his. 'You have to admit it doesn't look as though you need any ransom from my father to keep you going,' she murmured.

'No?' His glance met and held hers. 'Perhaps I have kidnapped you for your beautiful face?'

She was disconcerted by his words. 'I'm not so conceited as to think you are interested in me personally,' she said. 'Besides, you wouldn't have brought me here for that! Not with your mother here—and everything!' She moved restively beneath his gaze. 'So it has to be money!'

'You think too much about money, *cara*,' he rebuked

her. 'There are other things in life. I am glad to know, however, that you have decided you have nothing to fear from staying under my roof.'

'I didn't say that,' she argued. 'How should I know what horrors you have in store for me?'

'But you are hoping for the best?' he taunted her.

'I'm hoping you'll let me go!' she retorted, stung. As if she would ever want to be the object of his attentions! 'If you own a palace and come from such a long line of gentlemen, surely you're a gentleman yourself? I'm not afraid you'll either murder me, or rape me, if that's what you mean?'

He spread his hands in a gesture of fatality. 'Perhaps you should consider the possibility, Deborah Beaumont. I am a man before I am a gentleman—as were most of my ancestors, I believe.'

'I still don't think you'll murder me,' she said stiffly. 'And as for rape, if you're as easily tempted as all that, you should think twice before you send your minions out to capture hapless females who don't want to have anything to do with you!'

'Like yourself,' he murmured. 'It occurs to me you have been going out with this Michael of yours for too long. You may challenge him with impunity, but a real man is far more likely to conclude that you are asking for trouble.'

She gasped indignantly. 'How dare you? What do you expect me to do, I'd like to know?'

'I'd expect you not to put ideas into my head you can't begin to handle for a start,' he answered.

Fear licked through her veins. 'That's too much!' she protested. 'Why should I submit to being captured and——'

'Kissed?'

'Certainly not! I can finish my own sentence, if you don't mind! I was going to say captured and held here against my will!' she finished. 'Of course I'm frightened and—*angry*!'

His fingers bit into her shoulders. 'Are you afraid?'

Yes, she was! And she hated him too! She tore herself free of him and took a strategic step away from him towards the window.

'What if I am?'

His expression softened. 'You have no need to be afraid of anyone under my roof, *signorina*. Surely you know that?'

She felt hollow inside as she brushed her hair back off her face and attempted a rather feeble smile.

'I don't like being called *signorina*,' she objected. 'It's so—so foreign and Italian!'

'I am Italian,' he reminded her.

'Yes, I know.' She made a wry face. 'The noblest Roman of them all, I have no doubt, but that is hardly calculated to make me like it any better!'

He stood looking out the window into the small courtyard down below, his back to her. He looked strong and formidable from the rear and Deborah's spirits sank as she wondered what he was thinking.

'Shall I move you to another bedroom near my mother and sister?' he asked abruptly.

'So that I shall find it more difficult to escape?'

'Don't be a fool! So you will feel more at home here in the palace!'

'But I shall still try to escape,' she insisted. 'Not this afternoon, because I've promised I won't, but later on I shall keep on trying until I succeed!'

He turned and looked at her. 'Why?'

'Did you think I wouldn't?' she asked ironically.

41

'It seems to me most people would rather stay here in the palace as my guest than exist on bread and cheese and cheap wine in a student's flat somewhere in the city?'

'I'd rather be with my friends!' she maintained stubbornly.

'Friends who have to be paid to take care of you?'

That hurt. It hurt even more to remember how little Michael had actually done for her. He had passed her over to the chauffeur almost as though he had been glad to be rid of her. Perhaps none of them really cared whether she was there or not?

'I don't know that!' She tried to put a brave front on it, but her words sounded more than a little forlorn to her own ears. 'He may have had some other business with my father.'

'It's possible.' It was equally clear that Domenico Manzù didn't believe anything of the sort. 'But you won't find it easy to escape me, Debbie Beaumont. In any case, I should like to have your word again that you won't try to disappear this afternoon. You will find it tiresome while you are trying on your new clothes to have me too close to your side. You will have to choose between your desire to escape and your modesty. Which is it going to be?'

Deborah put off the moment of decision for as long as she could. 'Are we going shopping now?'

He put his head on one side, surveying her with a frankness that unnerved her. She shifted uncomfortably from one foot to the other, rubbing her fingers together.

'First we shall have your hair cut,' he decided. 'It is no longer fashionable to wear it long in Rome, pretty though it is. When it is short and properly shaped you

42

will look quite different—more sophisticated—and that will be no bad thing!'

'I don't want to have it cut!'

He shrugged. 'The victim of a kidnapping can't expect to have her own way in everything——'

'But it's *my* hair!'

He came close to her and putting out a hand tugged on one of her long locks. 'It will still be your crowning glory, I promise you that. If anything, you will be prettier than before.'

'That's not the point! I don't want to look pretty—not for you!'

'If you have your hair cut like a good girl, and don't run away until we have fitted you out with your own new wardrobe, I'll take you sight-seeing tomorrow and show you the very best of my city. Is it a bargain?'

She was tempted to remind him that she had already given him her word of honour, but she had no intention of allowing him to have his own way quite so easily. 'You don't have to *bribe* me——' she began.

'You will do it to please me?' he cut her off. 'That is a very pleasant thought, my dear. Do I have your promise you'll stay by my side for this afternoon at least?'

'That isn't what I was going to say. I'm too old to be bribed into good behaviour by anybody!' She carefully avoided meeting his eyes. 'I'm not going to promise anything!'

'Perhaps you are right,' he agreed at once. 'I shall be useful to you by doing up those awkward zips and advising you on the very latest in French underwear, about which I am considered something of an expert——'

'You won't do anything of the sort!'

43

'On the contrary. I shall enjoy myself extremely! There is much pleasure to be had in helping to choose——'

'You wouldn't!' her voice shook dangerously. 'Domenico, you wouldn't, would you?'

'Not if I have your promise not to escape from me today.'

'Very well, I promise—once more!' she murmured under her breath. She ought to be angry, she knew, but she felt more relieved than anything. It would be nice to be able to give her whole attention to the excitement of purchasing the new clothes he had decided she should have. She wondered if he had meant what he had said about French underwear. She had never worn such luxury items in her whole life and would never have considered such an extravagance if he had not held out the temptation to her. 'I won't need many underclothes,' she said, holding her breath in case he agreed with her, 'but I shall need some, and a nightdress, I suppose, and a petticoat, because I don't wear one with jeans, but it's different with a dress——'

'You will need several of everything,' he agreed with a promptness that she found highly satisfactory. 'Shoes too!'

'Italian shoes,' she said reverently. 'It will all be terribly expensive!'

'That need not concern you. Your father will be footing the bill and I am sure he will want you to have only the best.'

She made a face at him. 'You don't know Father!' The excitement bubbled within her all the same. 'Do you think it dreadful of me to want pretty things so badly when I can't pay for them myself?' she asked him almost humbly. 'I shall blame it all on you! I'd never have thought of buying French underwear for myself!'

'If it helps reconcile you to my hospitality it will be money well spent!' he averred.

Her face fell. 'You can't buy friendships. No matter how many lovely things you give me, I'll still try and escape as soon as I can. I'd rather not have anything if there are strings attached! My price is much higher than a few fripperies!'

He folded his arms across his chest, unmoved by her spurt of temper. 'How high?'

'Higher than you can afford!' she declared wildly.

'I wonder,' he said. 'But I am not trying to buy you now, so you can put your prickles away with a clear conscience.' His eyes settled on her lips which trembled slightly under his regard. 'Will it make you feel better if I tell you that I have never yet been in the position of having to buy what I want from a woman? I am unlikely to begin with you!'

'I *hate* you! I wasn't—— You misunderstood me deliberately! I was only talking about the way people make use of one and think it quite all right if they offer you some of their surplus wealth in exchange. There's no *affection* involved——'

He touched her cheek, exploring the line of her jaw with his forefinger and moving to her lips. 'Perhaps your pride prevented them from showing you much affection,' he suggested. 'Love and pride make uncomfortable bedfellows.'

'Sometimes pride is all one has left.'

'True, but don't expect more from people than they have to give, for it will hurt you more than them when they fail you.'

Deborah raised her eyes to his. 'But not if they really love me!'

'Perhaps not.'

'Would you fail someone you loved?'

His hand dropped to his side. 'Not intentionally. If I did, though, I should expect more from my beloved than hurt pride but perhaps your Michael is less demanding. Shall we go?'

He wasn't *her* Michael! So little was he hers that she resented having their names coupled together, yet only that morning she had been happy enough to be in his company. She threw her jacket over her shoulders, holding the collar together under her chin.

'I hope he is,' she said soberly 'He's a very nice person!' If she sounded more belligerent than she had any reason to be it was because she had remembered the cheque from her father made out in Michael's name. Was that hurt pride that made her feel humiliated by the discovery that Michael had been accepting money on her behalf? Well, if it was she couldn't help it; it would be a long time before she forgave either of them for the giving and accepting of such a sum over her head.

'There is such a thing as proper pride!' she told him. 'One needs one's self-respect!'

'Not between a man and his woman,' Domenico stated.

'I'm nobody's woman.' She sounded desolate and that was exactly how she felt.

Domenico gave her a little push towards the doorway. 'Poor Michael!' he said in her ear as she went past him.

'Why *poor* Michael? He's a great artist and he's going to be madly rich one day! He's always telling me so!'

46

'But he hasn't got you?'

'I don't know. He may have.'

Domenico laughed and the sound grated against her nerves. 'If you were mine you would know it in every fibre of your being. There would be no room for any doubt in your mind!' He said something else in Italian and although she didn't understand exactly what it was, she was glad she didn't have to answer him. Her whole being trembled under his touch as he guided her down the long corridors of the palace towards the front door. His hand had a possessive feel to it as it swept her along by his side.

'I thought men preferred long hair,' she said, finding the silence hard to put up with. He could *not* have said he wanted to make love to her! How could he have done so when he found her gauche and rather silly? She must have misunderstood him. It had to be that!

'I should prefer yours short. Short and curling all over your head.'

'It isn't *very* curly,' she almost apologised.

'Properly cut, it will be beautiful,' he soothed her. 'You will see, *cara mia*, how well it'll suit you! Won't you trust me in this?'

She managed a brief nod, her breath having been taken away by the pace he had set. 'I've never had short hair!' she said. 'Not even when I was a child! But I may like it after all.'

'Good,' he said.

She sat beside him in the car wondering at her own meekness. Should she have put up more of a battle before submitting to his edicts about her future appearance? She might have done had he been anyone else, but she was strangely vulnerable where this particular man was concerned. She tried to make up her mind whether she liked him very much, or wanted to put as much distance between them as she possibly could. Neither solution was entirely satisfactory to her, and yet what was the point of wanting both to be with him and never to see him again?

The hair salon to which he took her was much grander than anything she would have thought of for herself. Deborah was doubtful of the soft apricot lighting and the smart brittle attendants who escorted the customers from one scene of activity to the next. All of them spoke English but they might as well have not for all the heed they paid to her It was Domenico who commanded their attention a Domenico who made himself completely at home in the feminine surroundings in which he found himself and who directed the whole operation on Deborah's hair with a firmness of purpose that brooked no argument from anyone, certainly not from either the man who was nominally creating the new style or Deborah herself.

Her hair was washed cut alarmingly short with a razor, and blown dry in a matter of half an hour When it was done she looked completely different She would have been hard put to it to have recognised herself in a crowd. It was very stylish and completely feminine framing her face with a softness that her long hair had never given her Then her eye caught sight of the prices they were to be charged for the transformation and she visibly blenched.

'I can't think what my father will say!' she exclaimed, She turned her head to look up at Domenico. 'He is going to pay, isn't he?'

'Of course.'

'I think I ought to thank you all the same,' she said. 'Do you think I look nice?'

Amusement tugged at the corners of his lips. 'Very nice.'

They left the establishment in a glow of mutual good-will. Not that he was going to have his own way in everything. Deborah mentally decided but it pleased her to know as certainly as if he had told her so that he too was surprised at how well it had turned out and that he was looking at her with a new respect and significance. Before his very eyes she was turning from a pretty girl into a very lovely woman There were dangers attached to that. Deborah suspected, but she couldn't bring herself to regret the transformation whatever might happen to her in the future.

Coming out of the hairdressers Domenico took her arm and led her down towards the river.

'There is something here I want to show you,' he said. 'You remember I asked you if you had ever heard of the Mouth of Truth?'

'Yes, but I don't know anything about it. I told you I didn't.'

'It has a charming legend. If you put your hand in the mouth and tell a lie it will nip your fingers.'

Deborah put her hands behind her back. 'I'd like to see it——'

'But you're not going to try it out?'

She shook her head. 'I don't know what you may ask me. I might not want to tell the truth—not to you,' she said.

'At least you don't mock such an ancient institution! There was a man who did so, way back in the eighteenth century, and he put his hand in the mouth and was stung by a scorpion.'

Deborah's eyes opened wide. 'Did he die of it?'

Domenico shrugged. 'History doesn't relate. I doubt

49

he mocked La Bocca della Verità again.'

'No,' Deborah agreed with feeling. 'Have you ever tried it out yourself?'

'Never personally. Through the years my family have been known to make use of it to test the virtue of their wives. It has never been known to fail to detect an adulteress, which has always been the most popular test to which it has been put.'

Deborah shivered. 'Were the penalties very severe?' she asked. 'They can't have loved their wives much to put them to such a test.'

'Ah, but in those days it was a terrible disgrace to be cheated by one's wife. Suppose I had not been my father's son? Should I then have inherited his place in society and his possessions?'

'I don't know,' she admitted.

He smiled at her serious tone. 'Nowadays it's a joke, no more than that, *piccina*. Besides, it has never been known to punish the innocent!'

He led the way into the portico of St Mary in Cosmedin, one of the gems of medieval Rome. Deborah judged the austere but charming interior to date from about the eighth century, but she was not the expert that Michael was in ecclesiastical architecture. The Romanesque bell-tower was much later but, she thought, equally charming.

The Mouth of Truth stood on the left-hand side of the portico. Some time in its history a third of it had broken away and it had been cemented back together again, giving the marble mask a sinister look it had probably not had originally.

'What was it in the beginning?' she asked Domenico.

'A drain cover. Before there was a church here there

was a temple dedicated to Ceres. Who knows all that the face has seen in the past?'

Deborah touched the nose and the flaring nostrils, carefully avoiding the entrance to the mouth. 'It's a pagan thing to have in a church,' she remarked.

'We're a pagan people.'

'Are you?' She wondered that he should say such a thing. 'Because you believe in such things?'

He took her hand in his. 'So do you! Here, put your hand inside and tell me you would still prefer to be with your friends?'

But Deborah would not. 'Tomorrow I shall go back to them,' she declared. 'They'll be worried sick about me! What will you do if they've gone to the police and reported me missing?'

He spread his fingers against hers, noting how much smaller her hand was than his. 'I'm not afraid of the police—or your friends—not now I know you are content to be my prisoner for the time being.' He watched the indignation flare in her eyes. 'You must be content with your fate or you would not be afraid to put your hand in the mouth when you deny it!'

She was tempted to prove him wrong, but her courage failed her and she turned her back on the marble mask, refusing to contemplate its powers any longer.

'I thought we were going shopping?' she said stiffly.

Domenico put his own fingers into the Mouth of Truth. 'I have no difficulty in saying that I am enjoying having you as my prisoner. Will you really try to run away from me?'

She nodded violently. 'As soon as I possibly can!'

'Back to Michael?'

'Of course!'

His voice rang in her ears, gladdening her heart. 'You may try, *carina mia*, but what I have, I hold! Run as fast and as far as you can, but you will never escape me!'

For that afternoon, at least, she was not going to try. Out of sight of the Bocca della Verità, she wondered that she had not told the lie direct and flatly denied that she preferred Domenico's company to that of her friends. What could a piece of marble do to her? Did she think another scorpion might be lurking in its depths waiting for her to tell such a small fib and one which could only be expected from her under the circumstances?

Her new clothes delighted her. Domenico had allowed her to haver between one dress and another for a matter of moments and then recommended her to have the two. And he had added to her choices with a profligate hand, pulling out clothes at random from the racks until he was satisfied that she would be adequately clad on every possible occasion. He had done exactly the same in the shoe department. To Deborah, who had been shocked to discover that the lowest priced were at least thirty pounds, it had been a novel experience to walk out of the shop with at least six pairs neatly packaged for her future use.

'I'll never wear them all!' she had exclaimed, awed that he should think she might.

'Why not?' he had retorted.

'They're all beautiful, but *six* pairs!'

'It's all part of the plot,' he had told her. 'If you do run away, your six pairs of shoes will slow you up and it won't take me so long to find you!'

She was silent for a long moment after that. It would

be hard to part with her new possessions, but she would have to if she wanted to reassert her independence—and she did! She had to if she wanted to retain her self-respect!

She got into the car and screwed herself round to gaze on the packages Domenico had spread on the back seat. In her new clothes, she thought, she was a different person, someone whom one would not be surprised to see emerging from a palace, and yet inside she was just the same.

'Why did you kidnap me?' she asked. 'Whatever the ransom, it won't even begin to pay for all these things! Agnes will be simply furious!'

'Your father is known to be a very rich man. We have had a great deal about him in our papers recently.'

'But that has nothing to do with me!'

His eyes flickered over her shadowed face. 'Who is Agnes?'

She was surprised that he didn't know. 'She's my father's wife.' A gleeful look crossed her face, lighting up her eyes with laughter. 'I wish she could see me in my new clothes! Her eyes would fall out with sheer envy!'

Domenico started up the car. 'I gather you don't care much for your stepmother,' he said dryly.

'No, I don't. She's very beautiful, of course, but she's as hard as nails. I don't see her very often.'

'Nor your father either?'

She shook her head. 'He has a second family. I'm a part of his first marriage which he'd very much like to forget all about. That's why he won't pay any ransom for me. Why should he? Would you in his position?'

'I can't imagine you as my daughter, but if you were, yes, I should pay anything I was asked to get you safely

53

back. So will your father when he fully understands the situation. Though does it matter so much if he doesn't?'

Deborah thought of the cost of her new wardrobe. What would happen, she wondered, if he didn't pay? 'It matters to me,' she said.

'Why? The clothes are yours——'

'But I can't accept them from *you*! It wouldn't be proper!'

He laughed, putting his hand on hers which as well as giving her a funny feeling in the pit of her stomach, made her doubly nervous of his ability to steer his way through the quick-moving Roman traffic.

'Proper or not, the risk is mine, *piccina*. You may accept your new clothes with a clear conscience! How they are paid for is between your father and myself and is nothing to do with you. How could it be? You are the victim of the dastardly plot, not the villain of the piece!'

No, he was that! But he made a very charming villain, she thought, and the hero, if the hero was Michael, hadn't done much for her so far. She touched her newly cut hair and marvelled at herself. As a child she had always preferred the villain to the hero, but she wasn't a child any longer. She was a fully grown woman, and while Domenico Manzù might have captured her person, she would be a fool indeed if she allowed him to capture her heart.

CHAPTER FOUR

GIANETTA, Domenico's sister, was overjoyed to find Deborah was staying with them.

'We have been so dull these last few days!' she complained to the English girl. Her eyes sparkled with laughter at her own foolishness. 'The truth is that Cesare has been away.'

'Cesare is my future son-in-law,' her mother supplied. She looked Deborah up and down, carefully assessing her appearance. 'I thought you a pretty girl at lunchtime, but now I see you are beautiful, *signorina*. But I expect my son has already told you that! What are your plans for tomorrow?'

Deborah hesitated before replying. She was painfully conscious of her new appearance. Her long emerald skirts clung to her legs, revealing her shape in a way her jeans had never done. She knew she was looking extremely well, but she couldn't enjoy the feeling, not while she felt she had accepted her new glamour under false pretences. What would happen to all these clothes if her father refused to pay for them? Would Domenico be able to return them to the shops they had come from? She doubted it, not once they had been worn, and he had insisted that she should change for the evening meal as the rest of the household did. But she still felt guilty at obeying him with scarcely a protest passing her lips. She had wanted to wear her new things, and that, she knew, was a vanity she might rue dearly in the time to come. She knew her father and Domenico did not!

'I may not be here,' she said in reply. 'My friends will expect me to spend some of my time with them.'

'Friends?' the Signora repeated. 'You have friends in Rome?'

'I travelled with them,' Deborah told her, 'I didn't know I was going to stay here.'

'But if your father had arranged that you should stay with Domenico, why did no one think to tell you?' the Signora insisted.

'Deborah doesn't live with her father,' Domenico put in smoothly, not really explaining at all, but successfully diverting his family's attention from the point in question.

'Where *do* you live, child?' Signora Manzù's worst expectations of English family life seemed suddenly realised and she was plainly torn between triumph that the Italian way was so much better and genuine concern for her young guest who must have suffered the nameless horrors of a broken marriage.

'I live with my mother,' Deborah answered her.

'The poor soul! I feel for her in her loneliness! In my own case, my husband was taken from me by death, but I can understand her loss. You must be a great consolation to her.'

'My mother is fond of me,' Deborah agreed. 'But I think she was relieved to be free of my father when they decided to part company. I was too young to remember anything about it, but my mother has always been a happy sort of person——'

'Like her daughter?' Domenico interposed.

'I've always felt much more sorry for my father,' she added quickly.

'Ah yes,' Domenico said wisely. 'He has to live with the abominable Agnes!'

She was disconcerted. 'Well, yes,' she admitted. She remembered that her father was a business acquaintance of his and went on hastily, 'Not everyone dislikes her. She—she can make herself very pleasant. Perhaps you have met her?'

'I? No, never! I am content to have met your father's daughter. She is much more to my taste than his present wife, damned as she is with faint praise. The daughter interests me greatly, on the other hand, as I think she knows?'

Deborah shook her head. Her breath caught in her throat. The confidence of the man, to flirt with her under his mother's eyes, just as though she were an ordinary guest of the family, introduced by him because he wanted them to get to know her! Oh, how could he? How could he raise his mother's expectations as to her possible importance to him, when they both knew——

'She is not your usual style,' Gianetta said frankly, surveying her brother with a mockery so like his own that Deborah almost laughed.

'I have been taking a leaf out of her own book,' Domenico returned with a calmness Deborah could only envy. 'Didn't Michelangelo say the sculptor releases his statue from being imprisoned in the stone? He sees the finished result right from the start of the work? Well, so it has been with me and Deborah. I had only to see her to know what she could be, and now I have begun to create my vision of her, as we have spent the afternoon beginning to do.' He paused, smiling. 'Did you know that Deborah is a sculptor?'

'I am no Galatea to your Pygmalion!' Deborah denied, hot with indignation. 'Or was it the other way round?'

57

'Should I know these people?' Gianetta asked.

'No,' Deborah answered crossly. 'One of them was a statue whom the other one brought to life. But I am living flesh!'

'That I would be the last to deny!' Domenico said, smiling. 'More satisfactory in every way than a cold, dead statue!'

Deborah turned her head away. 'I don't know what you mean!'

Domenico brushed her bright curls with his open hand. 'One seldom wishes to kiss the lips of a statue.'

Deborah fastened her eyes on Signora Manzù's closed expression. She knew that her son's interest in their guest was unwelcome to the older woman, and that she could understand. She was a foreigner with different attitudes towards most of the things that mattered, an unknown quantity who could not be relied upon to behave in the traditional ways of Roman society. She longed to tell her that Domenico meant nothing to her, even to tell the truth, that he was holding her in the palace against her will, but she thought that that could only add to the Signora's misgivings, as it did to her own. *Why?* Why should Domenico have done such a thing?

Deborah was glad to find plenty of space between herself and her host at the dinner table. The refectory table at which they sat was at least twelve feet long and, as Domenico sat beside his mother on the long side, Gianetta and herself sat at either end in splendid isolation.

The food was every bit as good as it had been at lunchtime. Deborah refused the pasta dish with regret and almost immediately wished she hadn't as Signora Manzù could only suppose that to refuse good food was symptomatic of serious illness.

'You are tired, *signorina*?' she began her campaign.

'A little,' Deborah admitted. 'It's been a long and eventful day.'

Domenico looked up, his eyes meeting hers with a clash that she felt right down to her toes. 'Let's hope you have an uneventful night,' he said lightly. 'A good sleep and tomorrow you will be eating enough to satisfy my mother.'

'You should not have dragged her round the shops this afternoon!' his mother retorted. 'Didn't I say she should rest and compose herself?'

Domenico looked meaningly at the revealing bodice of Deborah's emerald dress. 'I am sure Deborah agrees that the result was worth the trouble,' he smiled.

'It was exciting, buying so many new things at once,' Deborah admitted. 'But I like my jeans too. They're very comfortable to wear.'

'But less good to look at,' Gianetta remarked. 'Mamma is always complaining if I wear such garments!'

'With reason,' her mother told her promptly. 'You have not the shape, *cara*. Deborah has the shape, but looked like a little girl. Now she looks a young lady and that is better, no?'

'Better than Alessandra?' Gianetta put in hopefully. She was rewarded by a strained silence from both members of her family.

'Who is Alessandra?' Deborah asked. 'It's such a pretty name!'

'Alessandra is Domenico's intended,' Gianetta answered. 'You could call her the girl next door. Her family's *palazzo* is the nearest one to ours, only her family were elevated by Napoleon and are much richer than we are. Mamma and I suspect it's her money that attracts Domenico more than anything else about her. She is—how do you say it in English?—she is not sympathetic to us. Like this Agnes you were speaking about!'

'Oh,' Deborah said.

'She is a friend of mine,' Domenico corrected his sister gravely. 'She is not yet my intended, though she would be very suitable for that position.'

'*Very!*' Gianetta put in irrepressibly. 'She is an only child and will inherit everything when her agèd father goes to the next world. When that happens, she and Domenico will be able to toss up every night to decide which of their palaces they will sleep in! Cesare and I are going to live in an ordinary villa,' she added with a smugness that made them all laugh.

Domenico stretched back in his chair. 'Palaces have the advantage of being large enough to escape from one's more depressing relatives!'

'Good!' said his mother. 'For live with Alessandra I will not!' Her soft dark eyes fell on Deborah with renewed pleasure, forgetting all about her being a foreigner for the moment. 'Gianetta is right—the girl has bad blood. It was rumoured that Napoleon's sister —but there, one cannot in charity speak of such things!'

Domenico's laughter filled the room. 'The damage is already done, *mamma mia*. Padre Umberto is going to be very disappointed in you!' He clicked his tongue in pretended disapproval. 'He will expect you to be doubly nice to Alessandra next time I invite her to our table.'

The Signora looked more mutinous than guilty. 'If

you give me sufficient warning I shall go out!' she declared.

Deborah wondered if Domenico really intended to marry this girl. He could not be in love with her, that was certain, or he would surely resent his family discussing her in such frank terms. But then Italians were known to marry without any love lost between them. It was a lowering thought and not even the prospect of his future happiness with the unknown Alessandra could lift the depression that had seized her in the last few minutes.

She put her knife and fork together on her plate and rose slowly to her feet. 'I really am very tired, *signora*. Will you forgive me if I go to my room now?'

The Signora rose also. 'You *are* unwell! Gianetta will come with you, *cara*, and see you have everything you need. Which room is she in, Domenico?'

'I put her in the one overlooking the Roman statues in the garden——'

'So far away from everyone else? Suppose she should need something in the night? She must be moved to the pink room next to Gianetta. You will please all sit down again and I shall arrange it myself!'

'No, Mamma. Deborah is quite happy where she is. If she needs anything, she has only to ring the bell and one of the maids will deal with her request. I'll take her upstairs while you are eating your dessert. Are you ready, Deborah?'

She nodded, a little embarrassed to find herself the centre of even such a small domestic contretemps. She felt Domenico's strong fingers on her elbow as she shook hands with the Signora and then with Gianetta. She hoped she looked less nervous than she felt as she murmured a '*Buona notte*,' in response to their wish

61

that she slept well after her tiring day.

'*A più tardi*,' Gianetta whispered in her ear, but her brother heard her.

'Not tonight you won't!' he growled at her. 'She'll still be here in the morning and you can gossip with her then. She won't want to listen to any more of your nonsense tonight!'

Deborah's eyes opened wide. 'On the contrary, I shall be pleased to see you, if I haven't fallen asleep.'

'I'll bring you a cup of coffee, shall I?' the Italian girl offered. 'I want to see your new dresses!'

'That'll be lovely.'

Deborah swept past Domenico and hurried through the door ahead of him, her head held high. If she could have remembered the way back to her bedroom, she would have told him to stay where he was, but the prospect of spending the next hour or so searching for the right wing of the palace made her hold her tongue.

'She won't let you escape,' Domenico said as they mounted the curved marble stairs to the next floor.

'How do you know?' she retorted. She noted with care the twists and turns he took to bring her to her own door, becoming suspicious when she could have sworn they had passed the same statue of the young Augustus for the second time. 'She will at least show me the way to the stairs without going round in circles!'

'Very acute!' he congratulated her. 'But you don't know what I have told her about you. I shall explain to her that it would be dangerous for you to go out alone in the streets of Rome. Goodnight, little one. Sleep well!'

'From now on I shall escape if I can!' she warned him.

'You may try! Goodnight, Deborah.'

Her eyes blurred with tears. She would have to try, but she didn't want to go. Ridiculous as it was, she wanted to stay within sight and sound of her captor.

'Goodnight,' she said.

Gianetta came with her coffee almost immediately.

'Domenico is like a cat on hot bricks,' she reported. 'He says your father is afraid you may be kidnapped while you're in Rome. It's happening all the time these day, but somehow one never thinks of it happening to someone one knows! Your father must be frightfully rich!'

'I've never thought about it,' Deborah admitted. 'I don't like feeling as though I'm Domenico's prisoner, though. Is there some way I could get out of the palace if I wanted to?'

'Only by unlocking the front door. The bolts are stiff with age, but you might manage it if you have strong fingers. Where would you go, though?'

Deborah smiled and sipped her coffee. 'I'd get a taxi and go to my friends.'

'You'd better ask Domenico to take you,' Gianetta decided for her. 'Do you like him?'

'I don't know him well enough to say,' Deborah said.

But Gianetta looked more than satisfied at her reaction. 'You'll hate Alessandra as much as we do when you meet her. Even Cesare, who never notices *anything*, says he'd like to wring her neck when she tells Domenico what he should be doing, and how he should behave to his mother and to me. I can't wait to see her face when she sees *you*!'

Deborah was less eager for the confrontation. 'Is Domenico really planning to marry her?'

'I wish I knew,' Gianetta sighed. 'But Domenico

doesn't tell Mamma and me anything we want to know. Friends tell us they see him out with lots of women, but he wouldn't marry any of them—if you know what I mean? Alessandra is so horribly suitable!'

'And will that be enough for him?'

Gianetta looked surprised by the question. 'What more should he want? It isn't the men who suffer in that kind of marriage, it's the women. When I wanted to marry Cesare everyone tried to stop me, but, as I told them, I couldn't have affairs with other men if I didn't much like my husband, could I? Cesare hasn't any money, and he isn't the sort of person we usually mix with socially, but I love him and he dotes on me! When Domenico said I could marry him after all, I thought I'd burst with joy. That's really why I don't want him to be landed with Alessandra. He deserves better than that!' She grinned happily at Deborah. 'I couldn't be more pleased about *your* arrival!' she added with relish. 'That's better than anything!'

Deborah smoothed the bedclothes over her knees. 'I already have a boy-friend' she informed the other girl. 'His name is Michael Doyle We're going to share a studio one day. He makes stained-glass windows——'

'You mean you're going to *marry* him?'

'Probably.'

'Does Domenico know?' asked Gianetta.

'I think so.'

'You only think so? He can't know he's important to you or he wouldn't have taken you shopping to buy clothes!'

'My—my father is paying for them,' Deborah explained.

'But it was Domenico's name on the cheque! Among our friends that's tantamount to a declaration of intent. You must have known that!'

'I didn't have much choice!' Deborah began hotly. She might have been even more indiscreet, but a knock on the door made both girls look round to see Domenico himself standing in the doorway.

His sister greeted him with a single-minded purpose that made Deborah shut her eyes, wishing they would both go away.

'Did you know Deborah is going to marry this Michael Doyle person?' Gianetta demanded.

'I doubt it will come to that,' Domenico returned with a calm Deborah could only despise.

'Why shouldn't it?' she threw at him, glowering at him across the room. 'I'm very fond of Michael!'

'Exactly.'

'And just what do you mean by that?' she insisted, throwing all caution to the winds.

His eyes were bright with laughter. 'I mean,' he said deliberately, 'that Michael is no more than a red herring! Fondness is a long way from love—and you are a long way from loving Michael! Isn't that the truth, *piccina*?'

Deborah stared at him. 'And how would you know that?' she asked him sweetly.

He didn't take the bait. 'One day I'll explain it to you,' he answered her. 'When we are alone and you have no one's skirts to hide behind.' He pulled his sister unceremoniously to her feet and pointed towards the door. 'It's time we left Deborah to catch up on her beauty sleep. She's had a busy day.' He came back to the bed and stood for a moment looking down at her. 'Is that one of the nightdresses we bought today?'

'Yes.' She couldn't have said anything else to save

65

her life. She pursed up her lips into a prim line and studiously avoided his eyes.

'Very nice too!' he commented. He wound one of her curls around his finger and smiled at her. 'Sweet dreams, little one. You have nothing to worry about now if you will only trust me.'

She clenched her fists beneath the bedclothes, fighting a grim battle against the effect he had on her. She muttered a stormy goodnight and turned her back on him, listening intently as he switched out the light by the door and shut it after him. She expelled her breath on a sigh, and then she heard it, she distinctly heard him turn the lock in her door.

She lay for a long time in the darkness wondering what she should do. It was, she admitted to herself, a temptation to stay exactly where she was. There were many attractions in being Domenico's prisoner, but none of them were likely to bode well for her in the long run. Yet how could she run away? She couldn't with honour take any of the clothes he had bought for her and she was reluctant, for reasons she wouldn't put a name to, to don her jeans and shirt again, leaving all her new possessions behind her.

It took her fully an hour to make up her mind that she really had no choice in the matter. She struggled out of bed and opened the shutters at the windows to admit the moonlight, then, moving as quietly as she could, she sought out her discarded clothes and dragged them on to her numbed body. Only then did she consider the best way to get out of her room, her heart thumping within her, beating out a rhythm of despair that she found even more demoralising than her own lack of enthusiasm for departing for ever from Domenico's palace.

The door was as firmly locked as she had known it would be. That left the window. It would be easy enough to climb down the wall to the courtyard below, she decided. Any cat-burglar could have done it! Ten years ago, she had been a better climber than any of the boys she knew, but since then she had been a non-competitor in such sports and she felt sadly out of practice. It was like riding a bicycle, she told herself, it was impossible to forget how to do it! But the longer she looked, the further down it seemed.

She had no difficulty climbing out on to the window-sill. Grasping the wooden frame she lowered her legs over the edge and searched with her toes for some of the footholds she had thought she could use when looking down from above. Her left foot found a solid piece of coping and, gasping with relief, she lowered herself a step further. The window directly below hers proved as useful as she had thought it would and a few seconds later she was hanging from its sill willing herself to leave go and free-fall down the last few feet to the courtyard.

'Let go, and I'll catch you!' a masculine voice bade her from below.

She lost her hold through sheer fright and fell heavily into Domenico's arms. 'How dared you be here!' she moaned against his hard chest. 'I might have been killed, scaring me silly like that!'

His hands tightened about her, shaking her until her teeth rattled. 'You could have been killed if I hadn't been here to catch you!' he retorted. 'That's solid concrete where you were planning to land! Did you think of that?'

'I thought I might break a leg——'

'Did you? And what would you have done then?

67

This courtyard doesn't lead anywhere except into my private rooms!'

'I thought you were in bed,' she exclaimed. 'If I could break in, I could have let myself out of the front door.'

'*Dio mio!*' he exclaimed. 'Do you hate being my prisoner so much? Does this Michael of yours have the key to your heart after all?'

She could not answer him. He held her tightly against him, pushing her face up to meet his with an urgent hand. For an endless moment his eyes searched hers in the darkness and then his lips were joined to hers, kissing her with an ardour that left her weak and breathless in his arms. A tide of passionate response rose within her in answer to his triumphant male challenge that threatened to take possession of her whole being. His hands slid down her back to her hips, pulling her closer still.

'Does your Michael kiss you like this—and this?' he questioned her. 'Dear God, I don't want to know if he does!'

She clung to him, conscious only of the demanding hardness of his lips as they commanded hers. She gasped and her senses reeled.

'Domenico——?'

He let her go, but only to look briefly down at her ashen face. 'Do I go too fast, my darling? You are right, we had better go inside where there are no eyes to see us!' His hands explored her with delight. 'How small you are!' he exclaimed.

'I haven't any shoes on.'

'None at all?' His laughter reverberated against her ribs. 'What have you got on, *carina*?'

She pulled away from him, tucking her shirt more

firmly into her jeans. 'I couldn't take any of the things you gave me,' she explained the poverty of her garments. 'I have other things in my suitcase——'

'If you are ever reunited with it! How did you think to find your friends with the whole of Rome to look for them in?'

'I have the address where we were all going to stay,' she protested. She turned anxious eyes on him. 'You must see that it's best I should go, Domenico. My father will never pay my ransom and you could get into terrible trouble for kidnapping me and—and I don't think I could bear that!'

He caught her by the wrist and pulled her after him through the french windows into what was obviously his study. A coal fire burned in the grate, giving out a welcome heat after the cool air from outside. There was a desk on one side of the room, on which were some papers that he had been working on when he had seen her feet appearing through the window. In front of the fire were two leather armchairs, dark with age, but as comfortable now as they had been when they had first been acquired in the latter days of Queen Victoria.

Domenico switched on a light over his desk and another one behind one of the chairs, snapping out the overhead with his free hand. Deborah made a small effort to reclaim her wrist from his hold, but his only response was to tighten the grasp of his fingers, pulling her round to face him. The shadows on his face gave him an arrogant look that sent her heart rushing into a new and painful tattoo of half joyful, half fearful anticipation.

'The clothes are yours!'

She shook her head. 'I can't accept them from you.

69

You must see that I can't! If my father pays for them, I'll wear them then.'

'You'll wear them now if I have to put them on you with my own hands!' he threatened her grimly.

'Domenico, I have to go!' she insisted.

'Back to Michael Doyle?'

'And to the others too. You must see that it's the best thing—for both of us!'

He sat down on the nearest chair, pulling her on to his knee with a firmness that came as a relief to her trembling limbs. She didn't object at all when he pushed her head back on to his shoulder and anchored her there with a loving hand.

'You had better forget all about Michael Doyle,' he said at last. 'If I had my way you'd never see him again!'

It was hard to think clearly about Michael or anyone else with his dark, Roman face so close to hers. If she stayed in the same room with Domenico any longer, she would never want to leave at all.

'I like Michael!' she said loudly.

His anger was every bit as exciting as she had expected it to be, but she could not allow him to cloud her judgment by kissing her again. 'Why won't you let me go?' she asked sadly.

'You ask me that?' he demanded. 'You ask me that *now*? Can't you feel how much I want you, sweetheart? If I had my way with you, would you still want to run away from me, back to this Michael of yours?'

She tossed her head in the air, breaking free of his restrictive hold on her. 'Why shouldn't I? It wouldn't change Alessandra's position in your life, would it? So why should it change Michael's in mine?'

Her heart missed a beat at the contemptuous look on

his face. 'He would accept you as his wife knowing you had already given yourself to another man?'

She shrugged her shoulders, trying not to cry. 'Why not? Alessandra must know she isn't the first woman in your life!'

Domenico tipped her off his knee and stood up, his face as bleak as she could have wished. 'Alessandra is better not discussed by you!' he bit out. 'I think you had best go back to your room, *signorina*, before the temptation to still your tongue becomes too much for me! I am trying to remember that you are a guest in my house and that your defences are unlikely to be as strong against me as you pretend. In fact I could bend you to my will as easily as that!' He flicked his fingers under her nose. 'Could I not, Miss Beaumont?'

'Yes,' she whispered, more scared than she liked to admit.

His expression softened. 'Yes,' he repeated after her. 'Remember that, *cara mia*, the next time you pit your strength against mine! You can only win if I allow you to!'

'But——'

He bent his head, brushing his lips against hers. 'There are no buts, Miss Beaumont. As my prisoner you must learn to do as you're told. Is it understood?'

And not try to escape again? Was she a coward not to even want to try?

'Yes, *signore*,' she said meekly, too meekly. Then she flung back her head and looked him straight in the eyes. 'But you can't stop me *thinking* about Michael!'

He smiled an ironic smile. 'You think not? I think I could, but I won't—not yet!' He opened the door for her and bowed to her as she preceded him out the door. 'Shall I take you back to your room?'

Deborah shook her head and fled. When she reached her room she tore off her clothes and climbed back into her brand new nightgown, burying her face thankfully into the soft pillows. But it was a long time before she slept. She turned on her side and wept bitterly for her lost illusions about Michael and men in general.

CHAPTER FIVE

It was raining in the morning. Deborah looked out at the dripping skies and marvelled inwardly that they should have caught her mood so exactly. *How was she going to face Domenico Manzù?* Her spirits quailed at the prospect. Domenico was like no one else she had ever met, or was ever likely to, and she hadn't the remotest idea how to cope with him.

It was easier to imagine Michael's reaction to the unpromising weather. He would take the pouring rain as a personal insult to himself, and there was something rather loveable about that. Domenico had no such comfortable idiosyncrasies for her to dwell on. He was as unyielding and as arrogant as the side of a mountain and she had never had much of a head for heights. If she had a little of his devastating confidence in himself she might have found an equal ability to deal with her own rebellious emotions before he had taken any desire to do so out of her hands with a masterful ease that made her breathless just to think about. No one had ever kissed her with such appalling effect, demanding a surrender her traitorous body had exulted in making. It was that that threatened to destroy her. A physical response to his lovemaking she could have understood, but she, unasked and unsought, would have presented him with her heart and mind as well. Only her pride had saved her from revelling in the new allegiance her whole being had discovered in his embrace—and this when she knew he was more than half engaged to marry Alessandra and that he was only passing the time of day with herself.

Be that as it may, somehow or other he had to be faced, and there seemed to be only one answer to that particular problem. She would pretend to herself that she was playing a part and was not really herself at all. She had all the props to hand: a palace, new clothes such as she had never worn before, and a prevailing sense of unreality that had persisted even in her dreams all through the long night that had followed her unsuccessful attempt to escape from the custody of Domenico Manzù! Domenico Manzù, she repeated dreamily to herself. Ah, there was a name to conjure with! It would take a poorer spirit than hers to have much difficulty in pretending that he, too, was nothing more than part of this episode of fantasy in which she had somehow become involved.

She wore a dress of navy-blue, with a Quaker collar and cuffs on the short sleeves. In it she looked slimmer than she did in jeans and, she was pleased to see, much less young and vulnerable than she had feared. Only her sea-green eyes, deep and mysterious, betrayed a lack of sophistication that at that moment she could only deplore. When she looked back at herself in the looking-glass, she looked scared stiff.

'*Dio mio!*' she taunted herself, remembering Domenico's exclamation of the night before. 'What more can he do to you?'

The unspoken answer brought a hot wave of colour to her face. Deborah didn't see herself as pretty at all in that moment. She was filled with exasperation that she couldn't better control her inner self. It had seen a governor it liked far better and her own inadequate measures to restore order were dismissed with the contempt they deserved.

'What am I going to do?' she asked herself.

Her mirror-image had no suggestions to make, except what amounted to cowardice in the face of the enemy, to ring for the maid and to ask to have her breakfast brought to her room. But, if she did that, how much harder would it be to face Domenico at lunchtime?

She snatched up her handbag, stuffing a lipstick into its empty spaces alongside her purse and a spare handkerchief, and raced for the stairs, giving herself no time to change her mind and cower in her room after all. Her high-heeled shoes sounded on the marble of the stairs and gave her something else to think about. She was unaccustomed to the sound of her footsteps echoing through such majestic spaces.

Gianetta heard her coming and smiled up at her. 'What a super dress! Did you choose it, or did that brother of mine?'

Deborah's expression froze. 'Does it matter?'

'Not a bit! You look a million dollars in it, whoever chose it!'

Deborah clutched the banister, discovering too late that its generous width forbade her stretching her hand across it. She lurched forward, retrieved her step with only a slight loss of dignity, and sailed down the rest of the stairs with her head held high.

'Domenico chose it! Naturally!'

'Naturally,' Gianetta agreed on a sigh. 'He has very good taste.'

Domenico had heard the exchange and was standing waiting for them in the dining room. He had his head on one side and his eyes were bright as he watched the two girls come into the room.

'I'm glad you approve my choice,' he said dryly to his sister. 'She looks charming, as I knew she would, but I think when we go on our sightseeing expedition she had better wear a hat.' His eyes met Deborah's. 'You will be able to hide behind the brim,' he added with a slight smile.

'Hide from whom?' she asked in creditably steady tones.

'From the men in your life?' he suggested, openly laughing at her.

She gave him a startled glance. Did he mean *Michael*? Belatedly, she remembered that she was his prisoner and that of course he didn't want to have her recognised by any of her friends.

'Two of them are girls,' she said foolishly.

'Ah, but you have no need to hide from them! Only from one man—one determined to be the only man in your life, and you will not hide from him for long!'

'Michael?' Her eyes darkened dramatically at the thought. She didn't want it to be Michael. Michael Doyle, who was he? She was beginning to think she had never known him at all, not in the way she had caught a glimpse of knowing Domenico, if only he were not otherwise engaged.

'No, not Michael. Michael is the crutch you refuse to

75

throw away because you won't admit that if you were to lean on him he would let you down. Where was he yesterday when you needed him?'

She had a vivid picture of Michael standing beside the airport bus with her suitcase in his hand, his mouth open with dismay, and making no effort to help her when she had needed it.

'He's smaller than you are!' She cast an uneasy glance at Gianetta, but the Italian girl seemed quite unsurprised by anything her brother might say to his involuntary guest. 'I didn't want to be taken away from my friends!' Deborah added loudly. 'Your brother practically kidnapped me!'

Gianetta laughed, comfortable in her belief that Deborah was joking. 'How romantic! I wish Cesare would kidnap me! I am tired of waiting for us to be married. There are so many relations to be considered and ancient traditions to be adhered to! I ask you, who wants to be married by a bishop in church, when they could be married in a register office tomorrow!'

Domenico put his hands on Deborah's shoulders and impelled her down on to her chair. 'I have ordered an English breakfast for you to make you feel at home, *piccina*. Have you any more complaints while I'm in the mood to set things right for you?'

She had a sudden urge to tell him to be rid of Alessandra, but of course that was impossible! She shook her head in silence. 'I have everything I want, thank you,' she muttered.

He released her reluctantly. 'I wish I had!' he riposted as he straightened up.

She wondered what he could possibly want that he didn't already have. And that reminded her of the ransom he hoped to get from her father for herself. He didn't seem to be short of money to her. Indeed, she couldn't think of anyone else she knew who had his breakfast served off silver platters and who drank his coffee out of a cup that even she knew was worth pounds rather than pence. Was it Copenhagen china? She opened her mouth to ask him, but thought better of it as a hot plate of the same design was put in front of her and a manservant offered her a dish of eggs and bacon, kidneys, and small pieces of fried bread. She took a conservative portion and thanked him, only to have the dish presented to her again.

'It's all for you,' Domenico told her.

'But I can't possibly!' she protested.

Domenico frowned. 'I have read that the English always eat such things for breakfast. At house-parties there are a choice of such dishes for the guests! Is it not cooked to your liking?'

Deborah's lips quivered. Quite suddenly the world seemed a much better place and she herself no longer like a fish out of water, gasping for breath.

'It looks delicious! Much better than anything I've ever been offered in England!' She picked up her knife and fork, lowering her eyes to her plate.

Domenico nodded to the servant, well satisfied. 'I want you to feel at home here, *cara*. After breakfast, I shall show you the palace. We are very proud of our family home and we have many things which will interest you——'

Gianetta screwed up her nose. 'If you want to live in a museum! Me, I shall be glad to live in an ordinary house without the responsibility of so many works of art!' An idea struck her, and her eyes danced as she grinned naughtily at her brother. 'If Deborah is a sculptor, you should commission something by her. She

77

could do a splendid bust of the head of the family!'

Deborah nearly dropped her knife and fork on the floor. Domenico's eyes flickered over her face in quick amusement.

'I shall be honoured,' he said.

'You don't have to be good-mannered about it——' Deborah began indignantly.

'Why not? You were good-mannered about the breakfast I provided for you I fancy the books I have read about England are a bit old-fashioned and that you no longer eat heavy breakfasts as your ancestors did?'

'Well, no,' she admitted. 'But you don't understand! I've only just stopped being an art student. I don't think I could do you justice Michael was not very encouraging over the last portrait bust I did.'

'I am unlikely to allow Michael to sway my opinion over any piece I choose to add to my collection,' Domenico told her.

Did he know how her fingers longed to fashion the clay into a replica of his features? Or would he want the bust to be of marble? She had never had enough money to use the very best materials for anything she had done. One or two pieces she had been allowed to cast in bronze and, until now that had been the pinnacle of her ambition. But to do a head of Domenico in marble! Marble from the same quarry that Michelangelo had used! She would be bound to ruin it—but supposing, just supposing that she didn't? Excitement stirred within her. Would he really allow her to do such a thing?

'You wouldn't have to pay me for it,' she said. 'Just for the materials. I could borrow some tools from——' She broke off, putting a nervous hand up to her mouth. 'Perhaps you'd rather I didn't?'

78

'You will have everything you need,' he promised. 'I suppose you want to choose the block of marble yourself?'

'May I?'

Gianetta looked from one to the other of them with astonishment. 'But, Deborah, are you sure you want to do this? Domenico's collection is famous! He has examples of all the most famous Italian masters. In such company——' She shrugged expressive shoulders.

Deborah's face fell. 'You're right,' she said. 'I'm no Leonardo da Vinci.'

'We don't live in the same age as Leonardo da Vinci,' Domenico put in. 'It would be surprising if you saw the world as he did.'

'Especially you!' Deborah's eyes opened wide. 'I mean——'

Domenico lifted a brow. 'That he was a man, and you are a woman?'

She was sure she hadn't meant anything of the kind! She had always held the theory that the sex of the person wielding the brush or the chisel mattered not a jot in the creation of a work of art. Why should it?

'The spirit of the age is different!' she claimed loftily.

'And Leonardo has not shared my kisses?'

'That has nothing to do with it! An artist's inspiration is above such considerations.' She was aware of sounding pompous and wished she had left well alone. 'It might have something to do with the way I see you,' she admitted reluctantly, 'but I was talking about a difference in style.'

Gianetta jumped up and down in her seat. 'Domenico! Did you really kiss her? It's too bad of you! When I think how angry you were with Cesare——'

Domenico turned and looked fully at her. 'Where is

79

Cesare?' he asked with dangerous calm.

'You know he has been away! But he's coming later this morning to take me out to lunch.' She gave her brother a subdued look. '*Mi scusi* Domenico.' She went on in rapid Italian until his implacable expression got the better of even her irrepressible spirits. 'But you were angry!' she accused him. 'And I wasn't alone and a guest in your house!' She peered at him through her lashes, a twinkle coming back to her eyes. 'You owe Deborah an apology more than I owe one to you!'

Domenico's eyes were inscrutable as he looked at Deborah. 'Do I owe you an apology?' he asked her.

She had no idea how to answer him. 'It doesn't matter,' she said finally. 'I didn't think anything of it.'

He had a way of looking down his nose that she found extremely disconcerting. 'No?' he said politely. He noted with satisfaction the quiver of emotion that passed over her face. 'Go and get your hat, Deborah, while I speak to Gianetta alone for a moment. It's only fair that you should see as much of Rome as possible during your stay with us.'

Was that an apology? She searched his expression, hoping for some sign that he was not going to be as distant and difficult as she feared all morning.

'You said you would show me the palace first,' she reminded him.

'So I will when I have made it clear to my sister your exact position in my household' he retorted. 'I will not have your presence here gossiped about, or remarked on in any way. She has embarrassed you, no, *piccola*? And that I will not have either!'

If she had, Deborah thought bitterly, it hadn't been half as bad as the demolition job he had done on her! Never, in her whole life, had anyone been able to shatter her with a single look, or destroy her calm with the merest touch.

'Gianetta didn't embarrass me,' she forced herself to say. 'You're making it all too important!'

'Am I?' He gave her a bland look that hid she knew not what. 'Does it matter so little to you what people think about you?'

'No,' she answered. 'But what should they think?'

He looked amused. 'If you won't concern yourself with your own reputation, you had best consider mine! Gianetta will tell you that there will be many tongues only too eager to wag about my offering someone such as yourself my hospitality. True, my mother is here to chaperon you, but it will soon be remarked that you have no one of your own to protect you. There won't be a soul left in Rome who won't believe I have kissed you at the very least, as I would any female, here, alone in my house!'

'Is it your reputation to be so indiscriminating?'

He threw back his head and laughed 'Bravo! But I will not have you belittle yourself, Deborah *mia*. A man would be very hard to please if he did not want to kiss you!'

Fascinated by the warm brown columns of his throat and the way his lips curled when he laughed, Deborah pulled herself together with an effort 'I don't care what they believe!' she declared. But she did and she knew that he knew it too. It was the way she had been brought up. It might be tiresome old-fashioned, even quaint, in these days of live and let live but she couldn't bring herself to believe that it did a girl any good to get herself talked about, though from all she had heard about Roman society, its members should have been the very last to cast stones at the *dolce vita*.

'You see how important it is how Gianetta explains your presence among us?' he pressed her.

'Yes.' Why should she worry? It was not as though she had chosen to be his guest. That had been his own idea!

'Good. Then may I suggest again you go and fetch your hat?'

She would have liked to have heard what he said to his sister, but his Italian was far too fast for her to keep up with. She turned in the doorway and looked at him over her shoulder.

'You could let me go,' she said.

He changed languages with that remarkable ease of the born linguist. 'I could,' he agreed. 'But how would I explain your absence to your father when he arrives to spend a few days in Rome with the daughter he sees so rarely? He would be deeply upset to find you gone!'

'My father?' She wrinkled her brow in confusion. 'My *father* is coming here?'

'As soon as he can get away from his business commitments. I spoke to him last night on the telephone and we agreed that it would be best for him to come here alone—without Agnes or any of his other children!'

'And he agreed?' Deborah could scarcely believe her ears.

'Of course.'

'I can't understand it!' she exclaimed. 'I never thought he would—— He scarcely *knows* me!'

'Or you him,' Domenico pointed out. 'A few days together will be good for both of you. You see what a good turn I have done you?'

'Oh no! That's too much! You'll be expecting me to *thank* you next for—for taking me away from my friends, and making me the object of gossip, and—and——'

'And buying you clothes, and introducing you to my friends, and of course, for kissing you in the courtyard last night!'

She wondered that he could be so brazen as to refer to it again! 'My father is paying for my clothes, and I have yet to meet any of your friends——'

His eyebrows rose at her mounting indignation. 'And the kisses?' he taunted her.

'You may have kissed me, but I most certainly didn't kiss you!' she came back. 'So what have I got to be grateful for in that?'

Panic spun through her veins again at the look in his eyes. She uttered a gasp of sheer fright that he might take it into his head to kiss her again then and there so that she might find out.

'If you didn't kiss me, what did you do?' he asked, holding her back from flight by the teasing impertinence of the question. 'Little fraud,' he added. 'Go and get your hat!'

She went. She was still shaking when she reached her room. She sank down on the bed, fighting to regain her cool. If she hadn't kissed him, what had she done? She repeated the question to herself several times and each time the answer looked worse to her. It might have been better to have invited his kisses when they hadn't mattered to her than to want them so badly now when he was unlikely to embrace her again. She wouldn't be climbing out of her bedroom window again, and she most certainly wouldn't be seeking other opportunities to be alone with him, so there simply wouldn't be any occasion for him to kiss her——

She caught herself up, dismayed at where her

83

thoughts were leading her. This was the man who had kidnapped her, humiliated her by forcing her to see Michael Doyle in a new and unwelcome light, and who, without doubt, was the most madly attractive man she had ever seen in her whole life!

And he had kissed her. He had kissed *her*! He had held her tight and he had kissed her as no other man had begun to do, and she had liked it. There was no hiding that from herself. Domenico Manzù had kissed her and she would never, never be the same again!

The hat that went best with her dress had a brim that drooped over one eye, and an imitation rose that nestled against the crown, adding a touch of romance that appealed to her. In these elegant clothes she had never looked more like a person of consequence. If only they helped her to bluff Domenico into thinking she was well able to take care of herself she would be more than satisfied.

Domenico certainly appreciated the hat.

'There's no danger of Michael recognising the old you in that!' he said with open satisfaction.

She was torn between claiming that Michael would recognise her in anything, because he was a friend of some standing which Domenico was not, and pretending that she hadn't heard him. She compromised by giving him a quelling look that made his lips twitch and lowered her head a fraction of an inch so that she could see him from under her hat, but he was at the disadvantage of being able only to see the rose and the fine navy blue straw of the crown.

'What do you want to do after you've seen the palace?' he asked her. 'I suppose you want to see the Sistine Chapel?'

'Yes, I do, but most of all I want to see the truly

Roman things.' She looked at him almost bluntly. 'I want to see the Forum, and the place where Julius Caesar was killed, and the Colosseum where the Christians were thrown to the lions.'

'A nice, bloodthirsty list,' he approved. 'We'd better do the Pantheon too, and then I'll take you to my own personal favourite among the churches of Rome, St Paul without the Walls, though I'm afraid you won't find any statues to appeal to you there. You ought to see the Pietà in St Peter's at least.'

'But not today,' she said, shaking her head. 'I don't want to see anything that'll influence the way I plan to tackle my bust of you. A strong diet of Michelangelo might ruin my own ideas. That's where Michael is awfully useful. His work is too far away from my own to get in my way, yet his advice is always good and to the point.'

'I see.' He sounded more disapproving than enlightened. 'And what does he get from you?'

'I don't know,' she admitted. 'I can never be as objective about things as he is.' She sighed, resentful that she should feel obliged to make the admission, but too honest not to put the record straight. 'I feel my art in my emotions and flesh. Michael's approach is all in his mind.'

'That's probably why you are a sculptor,' Domenico suggested. 'It's the most tactile of all the arts. One should always touch objects, don't you think? I hate being forbidden to feel statues with my hands.'

Deborah was astonished that he should understand so exactly what most appealed to her about sculpting as opposed to painting or any other medium. She smiled happily at him, delighted they should have so much in common. 'That's what it's all about!'

He laughed too. 'Come and look at my collection,' he invited her. 'I inherited most of the finest pieces, but I like to add to it every now and again. I promise you, you may touch whatever you like, and handle it to your heart's content!'

She knotted her fingers together, almost overcome by the urge to touch *him*, the strong, corded muscles of his neck and the hard line of his jaw, even the sensual moulding of his mouth. She looked away quickly. 'Have you any Roman things?' she asked him, saying the first thing that came into her head.

'A few. Perhaps their portraiture was better than the Greeks who tended to idealise their subjects, but I have to admit I prefer the movement and love of life that the Greeks alone perfected in the ancient world.'

Once again his judgment startled her. Was it possible that he knew more about his subject than she had allowed for, more perhaps than even Michael knew about the art of the long-gone centuries? She was used to accepting any opinion Michael might casually throw at her as true, but it was less easy to account for her undoubted eagerness to make Domenico's opinions her own. Had she no mind of her own? She gave him a helpless look. 'Are you some kind of an expert?' she demanded.

'I was brought up with the Manzù collection. It's quite famous in collecting circles, you know——'

Something clicked in her head and she could only stare at him with mounting awe. 'The Manzù collection! *You* own the Manzù collection? But how can you? I mean, everyone knows that it's worth millions! They put it on exhibition in New York! It's *famous*!'

'My dear girl, that is what I've been trying to tell you!'

'Well, now I'm listening,' she retorted. 'Only I can't believe what I'm hearing! If *you* own the whole Manzù collection, why on earth did you have to kidnap me?' She raised her eyes to his. 'Peanuts! What possible use could any ransom for me be to you?'

He had the audacity to smile at her. 'I hadn't thought of that. What do you want me to say? I kidnapped you! Isn't that enough to be going on with?'

'*No!*'

He shrugged his shoulders. 'I was afraid it wouldn't be. Would you believe that your father——' He broke off at the sound of a high-pitched feminine voice being greeted in the hall by Gianetta. 'Phew!' he exclaimed. 'Saved by the bell!' He ducked under the brim of her hat, and kissed her lightly on the cheek. 'You're still my prisoner!' he cautioned her, his eyes brilliant with laughter. 'Remember that!'

She wasn't likely to forget it!

'I think you have a visitor,' she said in a strained voice.

'Perhaps she'll be content with Gianetta——'

The door was flung open and a dumpy yet rather majestic figure stood in the entrance, her hands folded lightly over her stomach.

'Domenico, *caro*, I came at once as soon as I heard about your little problem. You should have told me yourself, and not left me to find out from gossips with nothing better to do with their time than talk about their betters, but I am willing to overlook your carelessness of my feelings this once! Men are always thoughtless when other people take advantage of them. I suspect they don't like people to guess they are much less able to protect themselves from the unscrupulous than they pretend! But really, Domenico, to allow people to say you are paying for some English girl's clothing is too much for me to swallow! You had only to ask me to accompany you and I should have made it my business to send her about her business! Why didn't you come to me?'

Domenico raised a quizzical brow. It hid a cold fury that Deborah would have died sooner than have brought on her own head, but this girl seemed not to notice. She turned a complacent smile on Deborah, brushing an imaginary speck of dust from the front of her skirt.

'I didn't ask you,' Domenico said slowly and clearly, 'because Deborah is my mother's guest, and my own, and stands in no need of your protection or anyone else's.' He took Deborah by the hand and led her forward, whether she would or no. 'Allow me to present Miss Deborah Beaumont, the eldest daughter of Edmund Beaumont of Beaumont International. The Signorina Donna Alessandra dell'Ameglia,' he turned to Deborah. 'Donna Alessandra is a neighbour of ours. Her father and mine were friends.'

Alessandra turned an unbecoming shade of red, recognising the snub. 'But we are friends also, Domenico,' she said.

He looked her up and down as though she were a stranger to him. 'We have been acquainted since childhood,' he acknowledged.

'Exactly!' said Alessandra. 'There are no friends like old friends, that have been tried and tested by time.'

CHAPTER SIX

ALESSANDRA went with them on their tour round the palace.

'It is older than ours, of course,' she told Deborah, 'but ours is very much grander. In medieval times their ideas of scale hadn't developed as they did later on.' Her disparaging tones caught Deborah on the raw.

'I suppose it's a matter of taste,' she said, there being no doubt which she herself preferred, 'but I shouldn't like my home to be thought ostentatious even if it were a palace.'

'One has a responsibility to one's family's history,' Alessandra shrugged. 'I am always telling Domenico what he owes to his family's name. I can't be expected to be forever rescuing him from every predicament he gets himself into.'

Deborah was doubly glad that her hat half-hid her face. 'Has he asked you to?' she inquired sweetly.

'Everyone knows how desirable a connection between our families would be. The Manzùs have never been sufficiently careful of their reputations, unfortunately, but no one has ever questioned that we have always been everything we ought. Papà and Mamma have always insisted that I maintain that tradition. *We* also are seen frequently at the Vatican, you know, and there has never been a word of scandal breathed about *us*, not even when half the better known families were getting involved in what came to be known as La Dolce Vita. Would we could say the same about the Manzùs!'

'But you can't?' Deborah encouraged her.

'No, one can't! Domenico's own mother—but there, it is not in my nature to gossip.'

Not now the damage has been done and the seed of suspicion sown, Deborah thought. She had no doubt at all that Alessandra had fallen behind Domenico quite deliberately, determined to make sure that Deborah understood her own position in Domenico's life. Her lack of interest in the English girl as a person was equally obvious.

Deborah struggled to maintain a sober front. 'Aren't you afraid that even your good influence may not be enough to make Domenico completely respectable?' she suggested, a little ashamed of herself even as she put the question.

Alessandra preened herself. 'Don't you believe that a good woman can work wonders?' she countered, completely serious. 'I have often heard sermons to that effect, and Papà says he would never be half the man he is were it not for Mamma!'

Deborah swallowed. 'Let's hope Domenico will say the same!'

'Why shouldn't he?' Alessandra smiled. 'He may have been wild in the past, but even he knows how impossible it would be for a Manzù to ally himself with, say, some commercial interest. The Roman nobility is not yet so debased that it has to go into trade!'

Domenico, who had turned and come back to them, heard the end of the Italian girl's remark and ground his teeth. 'We can't live in the past for ever!' he snapped at her. 'I've been a good Republican ever since I could walk!'

Alessandra smiled kindly at him. 'It doesn't matter to me that you don't use your title,' she assured him.

'Why should it? Everyone knows who you are, whether you use it or not!'

'True. My family had proud beginnings. Yours is full of pride now. Perhaps one can't have both?'

'We are not ashamed of our Napoleonic beginnings!' Alessandra averred, two angry red spots appearing in her cheeks.

'Personally, I find it difficult to forget that Bonaparte was a foreigner,' Domenico drawled. 'We would have been better off without him!'

Deborah didn't know why she should, but she felt a little sorry for Alessandra. She cast Domenico a reproachful glance, and changed the subject with a deftness that was rewarded by a look of distaste from Alessandra.

'Roman history is a closed book to me after the death of Julius Caesar,' she said. 'Please may we see your collection, *signore*, before I burst with excitement? Alessandra has probably seen it often, so it won't mean the same to her, but I can hardly wait to see if it's as beautiful as people say!'

'*Signore*? Are we being so formal?' he mocked her.

'Alessandra——' she began to explain.

'Donna Alessandra,' the Italian girl corrected her. 'I do use my title. I think it makes things clear from the beginning as to my position, don't you?'

'Possibly,' Deborah murmured.

'I knew you would,' Alessandra congratulated her. 'The English understand these things very well, so I have always been told. I am so glad that you have no designs to be thought better than you are. I have seen Domenico's collection several times, so you must forgive me if I leave you to see it by yourself. Now that I have met you I shall do my best to put an end to the talk

91

about you—so embarrassing for you! Anyone could see at a glance that you are not stupid enough to want to trap Domenico into any kind of relationship with you. Marriage, of course, is quite out of the question! But Domenico's reputation——' She shrugged her plump shoulders, spreading her hands to signify that she need say no more.

'Do go on, Sandra,' Domenico invited her.

She pouted up at him. 'You know I hate having my name shortened!' she rebuked him. 'And it isn't at all proper for me to know what you do with your female friends. *They* have nothing to do with *us*, have they? A dutiful wife——'

'But you are not my wife!'

Alessandra didn't even blink. 'We all know that, Domenico *caro*. Just as we all know you will have to marry some time and that you must have a suitable bride, as nobly born as yourself, to carry on the line.'

Domenico stared at her with distaste. 'Which particular line do you have in mind, Alessandra?'

'But that's the whole point!' she exclaimed, much as a governess would reprove a favourite charge. 'Both lines must continue, even if they have to merge to do so.'

Domenico looked as haughty as Deborah had ever seen him. 'I can only assure you, Alessandra, that that will never be my reason for contemplating matrimony. I am not a stallion to be put to stud, and I shall prefer my wife to have other qualities besides those of a brood mare——'

'*Domenico!* I will not be spoken of in such terms!'

Domenico's smile was formal and completely without any redeeming humour. 'Is that too coarse for you? But it was you, my dear, who would reduce marriage to the level of the stud farm. You must forgive me if I misunderstood you?'

'Domenico, it has always been understood——'

'Has it, my dear? By whom?'

'By both our families, for a start!'

His face softened. 'Would such a match be enough for you, Sandra? Is there to be no love in your life?'

'I love God! And I have been brought up to know that only by doing one's duty can one achieve happiness. I have few romantic notions, as you very well know.'

'You love God,' he repeated. 'You would be happier if you took the veil.'

'Without doubt. But it's my *duty*——'

'And mine too, it would seem. Unfortunately, I have inherited as much, if not more, from my mother than from my father. Duty and I are often strangers to one another. Don't rely on me, Alessandra, when it comes to duty!'

But Alessandra was no longer listening. She rearranged her clothing into immaculate order and smiled the smile of one who knows with absolute certainty that she is right. 'But I do,' she murmured. 'I always think the best of people if I possibly can. Mamma may think you weak, Domenico, but I would never allow such a thought to enter my mind!'

Domenico's face tightened. 'Your mother will be wondering where you are,' he said quite kindly. 'Do you mind if I don't see you to the door? Deborah has waited long enough for her viewing of the Manzù collection.'

Alessandra didn't mind at all. She nodded towards Deborah, making no attempt to take her outstretched hand. 'I shall probably not see you again,' she said, 'but

I hope you have a good journey back to England. Goodbye.'

Deborah watched her go, fighting with a strong desire to kick Domenico on the shins. How could he allow anyone to say such things to him, let alone that complacent creature? No wonder his mother and sister disliked her!

'Will you marry her?' she was horrified to hear herself demand of him, her mouth dry. Her tone was hard and brittle, and that shook her too. It was none of her business whom he married.

'She is, as she says, a most suitable bride,' he answered.

'I should hate to be anybody's duty!' Deborah declared. 'I don't believe in duty!' she added, wondering at the aching hurt inside her.

Domenico's eyes lit with sudden laughter. 'Don't you? When you marry, your husband may demand something of the kind from you! What will you offer him instead?'

Excitement stirred within her. 'Love?'

'That would be no more than your duty. He could demand your love!'

'Love is a gift, not a right,' she demurred.

'A man has a right to his wife's love,' he insisted. 'You can be sure my wife will be taught her duty in that respect!'

Was he laughing at her? She thought he was, but she couldn't be quite sure. If he intended marrying Alessandra he might wrest a kind of love from her, she supposed, but it would be a love of duty, never of himself!

'Poor Alessandra!' she sighed.

'Why? Most women are made for love. Why should

94

she be poor when she is fulfilling what destiny has made her?'

'I don't think her view of love is the same as yours,' she pointed out.

'I have no doubt,' he agreed promptly, too promptly for Deborah's comfort. 'Love is like any other art, you can feel it in your flesh, or think it in your mind, or occasionally combine the two. Alessandra and I will never see eye to eye on the subject, any more than you and Michael do!'

Stung, Deborah glared at him. 'Michael and I understand one another perfectly. We always have!' she claimed, defying him to contradict her.

'But then you are not in love with Michael, and you never could be. If you were, you would soon come to hate him for being content with a few kisses and a lot of talk! Michael will never take the trouble to master you, body and soul, and you won't be content with anything else in a lover!'

'You know nothing about Michael!' she argued. 'He's a very fine person!' But then what did she know about Michael herself? She had thought she had known him, but in the last two days she had been a lot less sure of their friendship. 'The finest man I know!' she added sharply, seeking to convince herself even more than him.

'I don't have to know Michael,' he answered. 'I know you, Deborah Beaumont. I know a great deal about you! You have a very revealing face, *carina*, and you don't like Alessandra dell'Ameglia one bit. Now, I wonder why not?'

She forbore to tell him that his family didn't like her either. 'I do like Michael, however,' she defended herself. 'And nobody has ever accused *him* of being weak!'

95

His smile accentuated the sensual cruelty of his mouth. 'Nor me, in any way that matters,' he dismissed Alessandra's implication with contempt. 'Now, come and look at the collection before I'm tempted to give you a taste of my metal. Enjoyable as that might be, I am trying to remember you are a guest in my house!'

She was both excited and afraid. 'I may have lived a much freer life, but I'm every bit as moral as Alessandra——' she began, afraid that he, too, saw her as Alessandra saw her, as someone he had no need to consider as a person in her own right.

'But much more of a woman,' he agreed calmly. 'I never doubted it, Deborah *mia*!'

And with that she had to be content. Only she couldn't help wishing that Alessandra had been less explicit about Domenico's future, or that she had been more so, and then perhaps Deborah would have a better understanding of what had driven Domenico into kidnapping herself. There were other things about him she would have liked to know too, but those things were better not examined too closely, not unless she wanted to find out something about herself at the same time—and that she did not! She preferred herself as she had always been, and that was the way she would stay. But there could be no going back to a time when she had not known Domenico. There lay the rub, she thought bitterly, and like any other blister it refused to go away or allow itself to be forgotten. She would have to put up with it as best she might and she was very much afraid that her best was not going to be good enough. Whatever she did, it seemed to her, she was bound to be hurt—and badly. It was not a prospect that anyone but a fool would look forward to, yet the excitement lingered on in her heart for the rest of the morning, and it had absolutely nothing to do with the glories of the Manzù collection.

The paintings and sculptures were such as she had never seen before. She revelled in the variety of the pieces and how one work seemed to complement the others, building up into a satisfying whole that sent her imagination flying in all directions at once.

'You're lucky to have got to know the collection gradually,' she told Domenico. 'Seeing it all at once is enough to blow one's mind!'

'You're welcome to come here by yourself whenever you want to,' he said. 'One day, you may come and find one of your own works have been added to the collection!'

'My bust of you?'

'Perhaps. You have sold other pieces, though, haven't you?'

'A few,' she admitted. 'But not to the galleries you're likely to deal with.' She put her hands behind her back, frowning at a sculpture of a female nude with a fierce concentration. 'I've seen her before!' She searched her memory for where she might have seen it and came up with an unexpected answer. 'It can't be!'

'It is. Alessandra has reason to disapprove of many of my family's wilder moments. That was one of my mother's.'

Deborah laughed. 'Who could possibly disapprove of anything so beautiful?' she told him. 'What a good-looking family you are!'

'So we are!' he agreed at once. 'Only Gianetta is more like my father in looks. Mamma was a renowned beauty in her day.'

Deborah examined the tiny statuette more closely. 'I love beautiful people!' she said with satisfaction. 'I shall enjoy doing a bust of you. I think it could become the best thing I've done—if it comes off. I have a feeling about it!'

She was conscious of his eyes on her face and lowered the brim of her hat to hide her enthusiasm from him in case he didn't understand that she was always excited about any new work she tackled.

'I have a feeling about it too,' he said.

Deborah was disappointed in the Pantheon. She was willing to admit it was an architectural marvel when put in the context of its time. The concrete dome, with the hole in the centre, designed to bring sky and worshipper together, was a rather dreary shade of browny-grey. And the hole, the crowning achievement of a considerable feat of engineering, meant that the rain poured in on to the marble floor, adding to the gloom of the interior.

She tried to imagine how the people of the first century had crowded inside the building, freed from the usual columns needed to keep the roof up, and had worshipped their strange gods. Now it was a church dedicated to the Virgin Mary and all the martys, but it had none of the atmosphere of a loved building. It was grand and remote and a little overpowering, but it failed to pull at her heart-strings. Not even the tomb of the painter Raphael, close behind that of his beloved fiancée, Maria da Bibiena, who preceded him by a few months into an early grave, could reconcile Deborah to the harshness of the great, circular empty space that dwarfed everything about it. Raphael was an artist she loved, but she could find no trace of him here to lighten her mood.

'I wish I liked it more!' she mourned, watching the

rain descending in muddy puddles on the marble floor. 'Perhaps if it were better lit———?'

'I doubt it.' Domenico was plainly amused by her reaction. 'Its splendour is mathematical rather than emotional.'

She nodded. 'Michael would appreciate it,' she said before she had thought, and then wished she had not. 'Though let's hope he comes when it's not raining,' she added hastily. 'Sloshing about in the wet doesn't help, does it?'

Domenico shrugged. 'Rome is often wet in the winter,' he said.

That was putting it mildly, Deborah thought as they came out of the building again and ran through the pouring rain to where Domenico had left his car. The water splashed down the surrounding walls and ran over the pavements, forming into rivers across the streets that in places were inches deep. Deborah had never seen rain like it.

She settled herself into the car, studying her damp feet with resignation. 'Domenico, money wasn't the reason why you kidnapped me, was it?'

'Wasn't it?'

'No.'

'So why?'

'That was my question,' she reminded him. 'I've thought and thought about it, and I can't understand it!'

He smiled. 'I couldn't resist it!' He turned her face to his with a finger under her chin. 'Do you mind being my prisoner?'

'I shall still try to escape! You can't keep me a prisoner for ever!'

'Perhaps not.' He put his lips close to hers and the

99

excitement burgeoned within her into a torrent that vied with the rain outside. 'How far will you run from me if I let you go?' he asked.

She shut her eyes. 'You'll find out!'

'But not today,' he mocked her. He let her go suddenly, putting both hands on the steering-wheel. 'Today we must pretend to be strangers, and you must see something of Rome. What do you think of my city?'

She nearly blurted out that she loved it, but she changed her mind. 'I'd like it better if the sun would come out,' she said.

'It will. I think we'll leave the Forum until it does, however. You'll have to content yourself with seeing more churches today. Shall we take a look at St Paul without the Walls?'

She nodded, not caring where they went. How far would she run? Her heart thumped within her as she considered the unwelcome truth that she didn't want to run at all.

'Did my father have anything to do with it?' she persisted. 'Domenico, there has to be some reason for you to—to take me away from my friends!'

'From Michael,' he put in carefully. 'But you don't need Michael as much as you thought you did, do you?'

'Then——'

'Forget it, Deborah. I saw you, I wanted you, and I took you! Isn't that enough for you?'

He put his hand over hers. 'I shall do my best not to hurt you, *piccina*. And I shan't let anyone else hurt you either! Does that make you feel better?'

'No. It may be you who gets hurt! Kidnapping is against the law and—and my father isn't a particularly forgiving man, at least, not according to my mother, and if he does give you any money, he'll make jolly sure he gets it back *and* that you pay through the nose for taking it in the first place.'

'You don't have to worry about me,' he answered her. 'Believe me, I know what I'm doing.'

'It sounds like it,' she told him wearily. 'Especially as you can't possibly *need* the money! In fact, I don't believe you want money at all! So what is it? Are you going to fix up a business deal with my father? Is that it?'

'That's a rather medieval way of putting it!' he smiled. 'I think we may come to some agreement, shall we say?'

'Yours is a medieval family,' she reminded him.

He smiled. 'Because we can trace our ancestry back to the coming of the Goths on a piece of paper? You had ancestors alive then too, my love, even if you can't put a name to them.'

'Alessandra wouldn't agree with you!'

'Alessandra has her own cross to carry,' he said ironically, 'and I am no Simon to help her with it. I find it sufficiently taxing not to be deliberately unkind.' He glanced at Deborah's puzzled expression. 'You don't understand what I'm talking about, do you?'

'No,' she admitted. 'What has Simon got to do with it?'

'*Dio mio!* I have found someone more pagan than myself!' he teased her. 'You would be better occupied in reading the Gospels than in worrying about my future and your own miseries, little one. Alessandra would certainly agree with that!'

Deborah bent her head. 'If you were talking about Simon of Cyrene, why didn't you say so?'

His eyes glinted with laughter. 'Perhaps because I

see you more in terms of Venus and the legendary gods of old?'

'I don't see you as Jupiter!' she retorted. 'More as Caesar, with his preoccupation about his wife having to be above suspicion!'

'She will be,' he said confidently, and she fell silent. How true that was, for who would ever accuse Alessandra of stepping off the straight and narrow way? She was, indeed, above suspicion!

Deborah loved everything about the church of St Paul. She didn't care that the original building had been destroyed by fire and the whole had been meticulously reconstructed in the nineteenth century. She loved the alabaster windows, the uncluttered interior with the portraits of the Popes around the walls, and the quiet insistence, backed now by the opinions of many leading historians, that this was the actual spot where St Paul had been beheaded and buried.

She was grateful to Domenico for not crowding her, or leading her from one item to another. Instead, he left her to discover the place for herself, talking himself to one of the priests whom he apparently knew slightly. Every now and again she heard his laugh ring out, and she turned her head to look at him, her heart thumping at the sight of him. She found it strange that they should talk so loudly in church, but Italians seldom lowered their voices and saw no reason not to acclaim the Pope, for example, with a thunder of applause, whether they were in church or not.

She was admiring a paschal candlestick, done, she thought, some time in the twelfth century, when she saw someone standing in the shadows quite close by her. She looked up, all thought of comparing the candlestick with the Roman triumphal columns gone from her mind. The outline of the man was very familiar.

'*Michael!*'

'Go away!' he said through his teeth.

'But, Michael, I only want to speak to you!'

He took a step forward, coming out of the shadows. He was looking awful, his clothes unkempt and his face unshaved.

'Speak to me?' he repeated. 'You knew where I was. You're better off where you are.' He looked her up and down significantly. 'A great deal better off from the look of you!'

'Oh, Michael, don't be like that,' she pleaded. 'My clothes don't make any difference to how I *feel*! If you didn't approve you shouldn't have let me go so easily!'

'Perhaps I didn't think you'd sell out to the enemy with quite such indecent haste,' he retorted. 'It seems you're your father's daughter after all!'

Her temper blazed. 'What do you mean by that?'

'Don't be naïve, Debbie! I'm no expert, but even I know when a woman is wearing the kind of money neither you nor I could earn in a year of constant effort. What did you have to give him in return?'

'Nothing,' she said stiffly. 'My father paid for my clothes.'

'Without a word of protest from you? Come off it, love. You're enjoying yourself!'

'What if I am?' she demanded. 'Do you have to be so resentful about it?'

Michael shrugged his shoulders. 'It's your life,' he agreed. 'But you can't have it both ways. Your father won't like old friendships getting in the way of your social progress, though, so perhaps we'd better say goodbye?'

'Just like that?' She thought about it for a moment.

'I don't think your hands are clean of my father's money either,' she said. 'What did he pay you five hundred pounds for, Michael?'

The expression on his face was ugly. 'How did you know about that?' he demanded.

'It was among your things you gave me to carry.'

'And you had to pry?'

'No, I didn't! I just came across it! But why, Michael? Why?'

He shook his head. 'It's best you don't know. It was something that was between your father and myself. You'd better go on back to your new life, Deborah. It looks as though he's waiting for you.'

Deborah turned her head, but she could see no sign of Domenico. 'Do you want to be rid of me?' she asked Michael. There was something new about him, she thought, something that had never been there before. It was almost as though he disliked her.

'Don't you see,' he said with a suppressed violence that startled her, 'that it can never be the same again! Your father's won! You *let* him win!'

She looked at him as though she had never seen him before. 'If I did it was because you wanted me to,' she said. 'You handed me over without a murmur. I felt like a pet lamb going to the slaughter——'

The sound in his throat was one of contempt. 'Some lamb! Grow up, Deborah Beaumont! It's you who've changed, not me! I'm still where I always was, as you can find out for yourself if you come and look me up before I leave Rome.'

That hurt as he had meant it to, but she refused to give him the pleasure of knowing it. She lowered her hat to hide her eyes from him and forced a smile to her lips.

104

'Same address?' she mocked him.

'I haven't anywhere else to go,' he returned with a bitterness that was distasteful to her. She didn't much like the new Michael—or was this the same old Michael and was it herself who had changed?

CHAPTER SEVEN

THE cloisters, Domenico told her, were by Vassaletto. It has small round arches on all four sides, with twin columns, some smooth, some spiral, and some with a plaited effect, or enriched with coloured marbles and glinting mosaics, reflecting a style more often to be seen in the Neapolitan and Sicilian schools of art.

'Who were you talking to, Deborah?' he went on, dropping the question into her silence as though he was quite indifferent to her answer.

'It wasn't anybody.' It might just as well have been someone without a name, she thought, for Michael had been a stranger to her.

'Nobody?' The question was as sharp as a whiplash about her ears. She cowered back from him despite herself.

'You already know who it was, so why ask?'

He looked more sad and disappointed than angry, and she began to think that with a little luck she might turn his thoughts back to the cloisters and the martyrdom of St Paul. 'Why here?' she murmured.

'Why not? I suppose you were bound to run into

him somewhere. It was Michael, I suppose.'

She nodded. 'But he was different. He looked awful.'

'Did you hope he would take you away from me?'

Tears started into her eyes. 'There was nothing personal in it,' she assured him. 'Only you must see it's better if—— He was so *peculiar*! Not at all like himself!' She wiped an errant tear away on the back of her hand, smudging her eye-shadow.

Domenico took her hands in his. 'What happened, *cara mia*? Didn't he want you after all?'

'It wasn't that! I never flattered myself that he did want me much, not in any way that counted. But he doesn't want me at all now. He said I was better off where I was. That I had sold out to my father and I couldn't have him too. Whatever could he have meant by that? He was ready enough to take that money! He made me feel *cheap*! You wouldn't understand!'

'Wouldn't I? You look very elegant to me, my love. But what interests me at the moment is where are your other friends? Weren't you all going to stay in Rome together?'

'In the apartment of a friend of someone we know,' she concurred. 'But the others were only going to doss there at night. Michael was included because of me. He's older than everyone else, but they like him well enough. Nobody could dislike Michael!'

Domenico looked amused. 'I could—quite easily!'

Her eyes widened. 'But you don't know anything about him! If he hadn't been one of the nicest people I know, I never would have considered sharing a studio with him.' Her brow wrinkled into a puzzled frown. 'We never talked much about the finances involved——' She broke off. 'The sun's coming out,' she said.

'I hope so, *carina*.' It was so softly said that she could have ignored it if she had wanted to. Deborah found she didn't. She welcomed the promise he held out to her like a drooping flower thirsting for water.

'Domenico, he couldn't have thought my father was going to pay for the studio, could he? He must have known that I wanted to do it all by myself! I've never asked my father for a penny, and I never shall!'

'I don't know,' Domenico answered. 'Would it matter very much to you?'

She wondered about that herself. She knew with a sudden certainty that she would never share a studio with Michael, if for no better reason than that she no longer wanted to. Was it possible that in the matter of a few hours she had grown out of him? The thought frightened her and she shivered.

'Cold?' Domenico asked her.

She shook her head, fearful that he might read her thoughts. 'Someone walked over my grave.' His blank expression made her laugh. 'It's an expression for when you get a feeling of foreboding you can't explain.'

'And Michael makes you feel like this?'

'Not usually. I've never had any worries about Michael before!'

Domenico ran his hand up one of the columns beside him and grinned at her. 'It might never have been raining,' he remarked. 'The sun is going to be quite hot for the next hour or so. Shall we go to the Roman Forum after all?'

'At least you won't be afraid I shall run away wherever we decide to go,' she pointed out, her bewilderment reflected in her sea-green eyes. 'If Michael doesn't want me, I have nowhere else to go!'

Domenico touched her lightly on the arm. 'Forget

Michael,' he advised her. 'You are more than welcome in the Manzù home, however you came to be there. You are a prized guest—as well as prisoner! Isn't that enough for you?'

It was, but she couldn't bring herself to tell him so. 'Alessandra doesn't think so,' she said.

'Alessandra isn't a Manzù,' he answered dryly.

She sighed. 'Not yet——'

'The Manzùs are all very happy to have you, Deborah *mia*. Both my mother and Gianetta would love you to stay for ever! They haven't led you to believe otherwise, have they?'

'No,' she admitted cautiously. 'But they wouldn't want me to stay if they thought it would get you into trouble.' She looked shyly at him. 'I could tell my father that you didn't kidnap me at all—that I came with you willingly! He might still pay for my clothes and everything.' She hesitated, her whole philosophy of independence overthrown before her eyes. 'If I asked him to,' she added grudgingly. 'He wouldn't even tell Agnes, if I asked him not to.'

His glance was remote. 'I wonder if you know what you're saying,' he said at last. 'Do you?'

'Agnes won't like his spending any money on me,' Deborah explained. Her courage wavered and fell before the look in her captor's eyes. 'Domenico, I don't want you to go to prison!'

'Most unlikely!' he answered.

'Is it? Don't the Italian police arrest people of your eminence——'

'Deborah, shut up! You don't know anything about our police.'

'Yes, I do!' she claimed. She grasped the subject eagerly, glad to be able to prove how much she knew about his country. Besides, she felt considerably safer discussing that subject than anything more personal to them both. 'You have three kinds of police; the *carabinieri*, a kind of military force who wear peculiar hats; the *polizia municipale*, who hand out traffic tickets and so on; and the *agenti* of the Commissario di Pubblico Sicurezza——'

'And what do you know about them?' he openly teased her.

'Not very much,' she admitted. 'But I'm quite sure it's better to keep out of their hands!'

'Very likely, sweetheart. But I don't need your protection from the consequences of my folly, whatever you may be thinking I've done. The police won't be interesting themselves in my affairs quite yet.'

'Are you sure?' She sounded as tentative as she felt, not knowing if she could believe him or not.

'As sure as I am of anything.' He moved and a ray of the sun fell across the austere lines of his face as his mouth relaxed into a faint smile. 'Quit worrying about things you can't help, Deborah. You'll be much happier without that Michael of yours when you've got used to the idea.'

'Will I?' She should have said something in Michael's defence, she supposed, but she could think of nothing that she wanted to say about him. The breathless excitement she felt in Domenico's presence, on the other hand, was becoming a necessity to her, and that had nothing to do with liking him at all. That had to do with being caught by his strong arms and kissed in a way that no one else had ever kissed her. 'I'm glad the sun's come out,' she said. 'I've always wanted to see the Roman Forum. Imagine treading in the footsteps of Julius Caesar!'

Domenico smiled. 'Shakespeare was not noted for his historical accuracy,' he warned her. 'The Forum was not where he was killed, but it is interesting nevertheless. For centuries it was the very heart of the Roman Empire, even when the centre of power had shifted eastwards to Constantinople.'

Her eyes fell before his. 'The British had hardly begun,' she murmured, 'as I'm sure Alessandra would point out if she were here.'

'I'm sure she would,' he agreed. His eyes narrowed. 'The Romans and the British have more in common than she would like to think. With a little trouble, we could understand one another very well!'

Deborah refused the challenge, aware only of her heart pounding within her. 'Let's not miss the sunshine,' she said quickly.

'Come on then, my little coward, I can wait!'

'Well, I can't,' she retorted, deliberately misunderstanding him. 'With only a few days in Rome——'

'What makes you think I shall let you go?'

Her eyelashes quivered against her cheeks. 'You can't keep me here for ever!'

He raised a mocking brow. 'You think not? Only time will tell which one of us is right about that!'

'Don't be ridiculous!' she said sharply. 'You'd do far better to think about your future with Alessandra!'

'And you would do better to hold your tongue on the subject of Alessandra, *bella mia*. She is not a subject I wish to hear on your lips again. Is it understood?'

'No, it's not! Good heavens, Domenico, what do you expect? I shall say what I please about her—and about anybody else too!'

'But not to me! I am weary of having the virtuous Alessandra flung in my face at every turn. I suspect you

110

do it to provoke me, but have a care you don't succeed and find the consequence more than you bargained for. I have never been known for my patience, Deborah Beaumont, and you strain it at every point, so have a care! I may hurt you without meaning to, and we would both be sorry for that, so let's hear no more of the sainted Alessandra!'

If his words were quelling, the look in his eyes was infinitely more so. Deborah swallowed. 'I'm not afraid of anything you can do to me!' she challenged him, flinging back her head to show him how little she cared.

He ran his finger down her nose. 'Then you should be!' He said something more in Italian of which she understood only the words *bella ragazza* and, because nobody would have called Alessandra a beautiful girl, she took it for granted that he was talking about herself.

'I'm not really beautiful,' she denied.

'Did I say you were?'

'I thought you did!'

'I did not. I said for two pins I would kiss you into a better frame of mind! *Pretty* girls——'

'That would have been in the plural!' she countered indignantly. 'You said *ragazza*—singular!—I heard you!'

'*Naturelmente*. A girl always hears what she wants to hear!'

'It wasn't a very good disguise, was it?' she said. 'Michael knew who I was at once.'

Domenico lifted her hat clean off her head. 'He found you unchanged?'

She tried to take it back from him, but he resisted the

attempt, watching the quick-change expressions flitting across her face.

'Did he find you the same Deborah he had always known?' he repeated the question.

She didn't know. All she knew was how much she had found Michael changed from the person she had thought she had known.

'*He* was different,' she said.

Domenico looked well satisfied. 'So are you, with or without your hat.' He put his head on one side, considering her. 'I think I prefer you without,' he said at length. 'We'll leave it in the car and let your hair blow free. Does that suit you, *mia bella ragazza*?'

She couldn't have answered him to save her life. There was no doubt that that *bella ragazza* applied to her, and he had said it with a deliberation that did the funniest things to her breathing and sent the blood racing through her veins. She touched her short hair in a shy gesture that was very appealing.

'Am I very different?' she asked. 'Not just the way I look——' She broke off. 'I'm not fishing for compliments!' she rushed on before he could accuse her of it. 'Only it was so strange seeing Michael like that and not really knowing him at all. We've been friends for ages!'

He took her hand in his, leading her through the church and out into the uncertain sunshine in the courtyard in front. Only then, when he held the door of the car open for her to get in, did he bend his head towards her, his eyes alight with laughter.

'I like the difference!' he said in her ear.

She smiled with pleasure. 'Michael didn't seem to notice.' She settled herself more comfortably in her seat. 'I wonder what he thought of those gorgeous alabaster windows?'

112

'Didn't you ask him?'

She shook her head, intent on her own thoughts. 'I'm worried about him!' she announced. She turned impulsively towards Domenico. 'Do you think I ought to go after him and find out what's wrong?' She thought for a moment. 'I could give him back that cheque. Perhaps he hasn't any money.'

Domenico tapped her sharply on the knuckles. 'That is not your concern, Deborah. You are better off without him!'

'Am I?' she said wearily, rubbing her hand. 'How do you know? I don't trust you either, if you want to know!'

'I'm glad to hear it!' His smile seared her spirits, but the excitement was still there, refusing to leave her no matter how unkind he was. 'But you are still my prisoner, little one, and you have no choice but to come with me. Michael will have to do without you!'

She stared straight ahead of her, maintaining an icy silence all the way across the city to the Roman Forum. There was some difficulty in parking the car, and once this had been achieved and she had her first glimpse of the ruined centre of the world, she forgot her wrath and chagrin in the immediate satisfaction of a long and dearly held ambition to see this place for herself.

Ignoring her pleased recognition of Trajan's Arch, Domenico bought their entrance tickets and then, taking her firmly by the arm, led her down the steps to the lower level of the city as it had been all those centuries before.

'I'm afraid you'll get your feet wet,' he remarked as they gained the bottom of the steps.

'But worth it!' she said at once. She remembered belatedly that he had paid for them and what they had

113

cost. 'I'll try to keep out of the worst of the puddles,' she added. 'I don't think they'll stain.'

'I was thinking of your comfort, my dear Deborah. Those shoes are pretty, but not very substantial. Perhaps we should have bought you some Wellington boots!'

She resisted the impulse to ask him whether Alessandra, that arch admirer of the Emperor Napoleon, ever wore such things. Alessandra, she reminded herself, was a banned topic of conversation between them, and he probably wouldn't have appreciated the joke anyway.

'Tell me about the Vestal Virgins,' she said instead. 'Didn't they have their temple here?'

'Yes, it's that round building over there. Their house is just beside it.'

And there it was, the fine brickwork stripped of most of its marble, but still quite recognisable in shape and layout. Deborah almost ran in her eagerness to examine the statues that lined the edges of the pool where once these important ladies had bathed and relaxed together.

'Why were they so important?' she asked Domenico, striving to hide the fact that she was really rather disappointed by the few, mostly headless, torsos that remained.

'I daresay politics had a lot to do with it,' he answered. 'And fire has always been a potent symbolism. To begin with, the Romans were far less inclined to personalise their gods than were the Greeks. We preferred impersonal spirits and powers, and Vesta probably began life as a *numen* in the traditional Roman manner. Ovid declared her to be "nothing but a living flame". But we soon came under the influence of the

114

Greeks and began to identify our own deities with theirs, taking over their mythology and genealogies as well as their humanised personalities. Somehow Vesta, despite her essentially impersonal quality, was associated with Hestia. the Greek goddess of the hearth. This was the hearth of Rome and, because the flame was never allowed to fail and go out, lest the power of Rome flickered and died with it, there had to be attendants to keep watch over the flame, and these were the Vestal Virgins. Gradually, all sorts of important things were left in their care, from Julius Caesar's will to the sacred Palladium, an effigy of Pallas Athene, known to the Romans as Minerva, which had been rescued from the flames of Troy by Aeneas and brought here to Italy.'

'Did they look after it well?' Deborah asked.

'It's impossible to tell. No one was allowed to see these sacred symbols except the Virgins and the Chief Priest. There was one awful moment when the Emperor Elagabalus, who came from Syria, wanted to make his own god the principal divinity of Rome. He decided to marry Vesta off to his own god, but, worse still, he wanted to carry off the sacred fire and the jar that held the Palladium as well. The Vestal Virgins claimed later that they had tricked the Emperor by handing over an empty jar, but it may have been just a face-saving move based on the current belief that they kept two jars in the Storehouse to confuse possible thieves.'

'But you think they were guarding nothing in the first place?'

'Not the flame. That was the central symbol of Rome, but I doubt there ever was a Sacred Palladium. Its importance lay entirely in building up the prestige of the Virgins themselves as its guardians.'

Deborah digested this in silence. Then she laughed, her good intentions all forgotten.

'Is that why you think Alessandra would have made a good candidate?' she asked, her eyes bright with the thought. 'Do you think her sacred family name as empty of value as the urn was empty of the Palladium?'

As soon as she had spoken, she knew her mistake. She knew it by the sudden stiffening of his back and his deliberately expressionless face. They might as well have been alone in Rome, for there was no one else to be seen anywhere in the Forum. His hands shot out and gathered her up against his chest.

'I warned you, sweet Deborah,' he said through clenched teeth. 'Why can't you forget Alessandra? Must you drag her into everything? And if it isn't her, it's Michael Doyle!'

'I'm sorry. Domenico, please, I've said I'm sorry!'

It wasn't anger she saw in his face, but she was afraid all the same. She was afraid of him, but she was even more afraid of the leaping joy within her that exulted in his touch whatever the cause.

He ran his fingers through her short hair, pulling her closer still. She swallowed hard. 'Domenico, I've said I'm sorry,' she repeated. Her voice trembled dangerously, betraying her outwardly calm appearance.

'Why are you sorry?' he murmured. 'Don't you know I've been wanting this all day?'

'But not with me!' she said.

'Why not with you? Did you suppose I wouldn't answer the challenge you are constantly offering me? Isn't that why you couldn't resist mentioning Alessandra just once more, to see what I would do?'

'*No!* Truly, it wasn't! I'd forgotten——'

'Deborah, *cara mia*, I don't believe a word of it!'

116

'But you *must*!' She gazed at him, her eyes darkened by the strength of the emotions doing battle within her. 'I won't ever mention her name again!' she promised rashly.

His lips touched hers fleetingly, his breath warm against her cheek. 'And Michael?'

'Michael?'

'*Your* Michael,' he insisted ruthlessly. 'Don't sound as though you've never heard of him!'

Deborah found it increasingly difficult to concentrate on anything but the closeness of his face to hers. The smell of his skin filled her nostrils, intoxicating her further. She shut her eyes, alarmed by the ease with which he could seduce her senses, but her will refused to answer her signal of distress, preferring a new and much more exciting master. When he finally kissed her, it was a shattering experience and her response was absolute. His arms tightened about her willing body and if she had not been clinging to him with her arms looped around his neck, she would have fallen, such was the weakness of her knees.

'Well?'

She made no attempt to answer him. She wanted him to kiss her again. She arched her body closer still to his, seeking a reassurance he was not prepared to give her. His hair felt rough and essentially masculine beneath her fingers. It was strange to think that she had never touched Michael's hair—had no idea of how he smelt or tasted either. Her whole world was filled by Domenico Manzù and, for the moment, she was more than happy to have it so. But, she remembered belatedly, it wouldn't do!

'Please, *don't*!' The words didn't seem to come from her at all.

117

'No? Don't you like me to touch you—to kiss you?'

Her only answer was a soft murmur of protest against his neck. His hands imprisoned her face, making it more freely available for his kisses.

'Little fraud! You like this as much as I do!'

She opened her eyes and stared at him. 'That doesn't make it any better!' she said. 'Besides, you're creasing my coat!'

'Damn your coat!'

'Domenico, it isn't right!' she protested.

He swore with a facility that startled her. 'Spare me your maidenly reservations! It's too late for that, Deborah Beaumont. It's far too late for you to pretend that this is some novel thrill for you, or that you and Michael Doyle have never shared such moments together! I'm sorry if you don't like it, for I have every intention of kissing you again and, as my prisoner, *carissima*, you must expect to suffer a little!'

She struggled in earnest then. 'Let me go!'

'Where will you go? Michael won't let you run to him!'

She pounded her fists against his chest. '*Domenico*, be sensible——'

He let her go too suddenly for her to retain her balance and she slipped on the wet ground, tumbling painfully at his feet.

'Now look what you've done!'

He was on his knees beside her in an instant. 'Deborah, *piccola*, have I hurt you?'

She was too honest to claim injury when the only part of her that was smarting was her pride. 'No,' she said grudgingly. 'But you've *ruined* my new clothes! It would serve you right if I made you pay to have them cleaned!'

He grinned, his hands warm as they clasped her through the material of her dress. 'Your face is splashed with mud,' he told her, 'and I should probably have paid for the cleaning anyway.' He cupped her face in one hand. 'You look very young and innocent with a dirty face. It suits you.'

It seemed she could never be angry with him for long. 'I am young and innocent——'

'Are you?'

He asked it as if he had some right to know, as if in some way she were his property and it was only good husbandry to check her over in any way he liked.

'Of course!' She cleared her throat with difficulty. 'Let me up!' she commanded in slightly stronger tones.

'I like you the way you are,' he retorted, making no move at all.

'Yes, but——'

He frowned. 'Deborah, are you playing with me?'

The excitement and the anger came together in an explosion that shook her. Tears flowed down her face and she was suddenly too weary to hide them from him. 'I don't understand you at all! I don't understand *anything*! I suppose it's quite all right if *you* play with *my* feelings, knowing you don't care anything for me—not really! Why don't you leave me alone and go and kiss Alessandra!'

The forbidden name hung between them for fully a second. It was the longest second in Deborah's life. Then, as his words slowly came through to her, distress gave way to an open-mouthed surprise.

'I am not given to kissing Alessandra,' he said.

'Aren't you?' she said doubtfully.

He shook his head. 'She hasn't your talent for making

119

me forget my better self until I don't know whether to thump you or make violent love to you!' Usually his English was as perfect as her own, with only the very faintest accent adding colour to his speech, but his 't'ump' was too much for her gravity.

'I think "t'umping" might be safer!' she said with feeling, trying not to laugh.

He shrugged his shoulders. 'It would end the same way. Deborah, may I kiss you again?'

Her amusement died. She looked back at him differently, as unsure of herself as she was of him.

'Why me?' she asked. 'You must know many other women——' She came to an abrupt halt as her heart took off on a new flight of fancy, swooping, like some half-fledged bird caught in an unexpected gale, into the air and falling inelegantly back to earth as often as it made the attempt. Did it matter *why* he wanted to kiss her?

'And you have Michael!' he sighed.

'*Michael?* Don't be silly!' she snapped.

To her disappointment he seemed to change his mind. He stood up over her, putting his hands in her armpits, and lifted her up on to her feet as easily as if she had been a child.

'*Bene, signorina*, we had better go home,' he said. 'This is not the way I had planned for you to see Rome.'

She could have wept at his change of mood, or stamped her feet, or torn her pinny, but she was afraid that if she did he would guess something of what he had done to her. How dared he trifle with her affections? she demanded of herself, smiling a little at the old-fashioned thought. She raised her eyes to his and faltered in her step.

'But you hadn't planned for me to see Rome at all, had you?' she demanded.

He smiled. 'Hadn't I?' His hand grasped the point of her chin and he kissed her hard on the mouth. 'Prisoners shouldn't ask too many questions,' he said.

And with that she had to be content. She asked herself a dozen different questions all the way back to the Manzù palace, but she lacked the courage to try any of them out on him. She was still fretting at the possible answers when he drove in through the ornate gate beside the palace and reached across her to open her door.

'It will be all right, Deborah. Won't you believe that?'

She had no idea what she might have answered, for at that moment a man came out of a door in the building behind them and walked down the few steps into the courtyard. Her eyes widened and her blood froze within her. *It was her father!*

CHAPTER EIGHT

'Father! Whatever are you doing here?'

Her father came across the courtyard towards the car, made a gesture as if he were about to embrace her, and then changed his mind, looking mildly embarrassed instead.

'You look a mess!' he said. 'What have you been doing to yourself? The idea was to get you out of those abominable jeans I last saw you in, but, if possible, you look worse than ever.'

'Thank you, Father,' she murmured deeply. Then the import of what he had said came to her more slowly. 'You know about my new clothes!' she exclaimed.

'My dear child, how else did you suppose the shops let you go away with hundreds of pounds' worth of stuff?'

'I thought——' Deborah cast accusing eyes on Domenico. 'I suppose you knew I was staying here too?' She sounded defeated, but her father didn't seem to notice.

'I hope you have something else to wear,' he said with distaste. 'You'd better go and change, dear.' He dismissed her quite kindly, but just as though she were still the small girl he had known before he and her mother had gone their separate ways.

Deborah stiffened. 'I want to hear why you're here first!'

'When you look more the thing, Debbie, I'll be pleased to tell you anything you want to know, but not while you're looking such a mess. What have you been doing? You look as though you've been having a romp in a muddy field——'

That was close enough to the truth to sting. 'I'm not a clothes-horse, nor am I like Agnes, with never a hair out of place and her stockings always straight!'

Her father's mouth compressed into a straight line. 'You could do worse than take Agnes as a model for your adult behaviour. Be careful that you don't try to remain a child all your life—like your mother!'

'I won't listen to a word against my mother!'

Her father sighed. 'No, of course not. Nor did I

mean to criticise her. If we're to get to know each other better, my dear, perhaps we had better start with a clean slate. I shan't mention your mother again and you must try to be equally circumspect about Agnes —whom you don't really know at all, do you?'

Deborah was silent. She didn't like her father's attitude, nor did did she like his implication that while she scarcely knew his second wife at all, she couldn't make the same statement about him. He had known her mother very well indeed—he must have done to have been married to her!—and yet wasn't it possible that he still saw her as she had been then, making no allowance for the changes that passing years must bring?

More even than that, he made her feel the impossible child he thought her thus, somehow, depriving her of the right to answer him back as an equal.

'I didn't ask you to buy me anything!' she pointed out. 'I'll pay you back every penny for them!'

He was as appalled as she by her outburst. 'My dear girl, I didn't come to Rome to quarrel with you,' he said awkwardly.

'No? Why did you come?'

Her father turned to include Domenico in the conversation. He looked more bewildered than she had ever seen him before.

'*Signore*, wasn't my daughter expecting me?' he asked him.

Domenico looked amused. 'I think not,' he answered. 'She was rather a—reluctant guest in my house——'

'He kidnapped me!' Deborah interrupted him.

Her father looked more confused than ever. Only Domenico remained completely calm. 'I had not expected you to get away so soon, Mr Beaumont. Your daughter and I are only beginning to get to know each

123

other and I'm afraid it is my fault that she tumbled in the mud at the Roman Forum. You must not scold her for that! But I am neglecting my duties as host. You will want to speak to each other alone, no? You must make use of my study.' He glanced at his watch. 'I have another engagement in any case, so there will be no one to disturb you. Shall I show you the way?'

Deborah looked down at her muddy dress and coat. 'I'd better change first,' she muttered, the light of mutiny still in her eyes.

Domenico gave her an amused smile. 'Wear the greeny-grey dress, *cara*. It will give your father pleasure to see you in something that suits you so well.'

It was her turn to be uncertain. 'Where are you going?' she asked him. She didn't want to be alone with her father! Couldn't he see that?

'I shall be back this evening, Deborah. Entertain your father for me until then, and save your anger for me, if you can, as my shoulders are broader than his where you are concerned.'

Deborah frowned at him. 'Am I going to be angry?'

He tapped her cheek, still smiling. 'I think you might be, but not with your father. The crime, if crime it was, was all mine! And you will still be my prisoner whatever you may think, and so I warn you!'

'Warn me?' she repeated, immediately suspicious.

'A captor has whatever rights he chooses to take,' he informed her. 'Now you are no longer alone and at my mercy, I shall have no qualms as to what I can ask from you!'

She refused to meet the warmth of his regard. She was angry now, she told herself. There had to be some explanation for the fluttery feeling inside her and the delicious panic that raced in her blood whenever he came close to her.

'You have first to prove yourself my captor,' she said calmly. 'I'm not convinced that I have anything to fear from you, *signore*, now that my father is here.'

'If you want his protection you will have to be very nice to him! All he wanted was a chance to get to know his eldest daughter.'

'And you? What did you want?' she challenged him.

'I wonder,' he said. 'Go and change, *carina*. I will take your father to my study. If you want to offer him tea, or some other refreshment, you have only to ring the bell. I would ask my mother to act as hostess, but your father will want you to himself.' He touched a lock of her hair. 'You can fight all you want with me later!'

She would certainly have an explanation from him before she was much older, she vowed. Her father, she suspected, was as confused as she was herself. Yet he had known where she was and, apparently, he had ordered that she was to have new clothes—but not a new haircut! Surely that had been Domenico's own idea!

She put up a hand and her fingers touched his in her hair. She drew back as if he had stung her. 'You should have told me,' she reproached him.

'Would it have helped?'

'I don't know,' she admitted. 'It might have done.'

'Not really,' he contradicted her. 'If we went to the Mouth of Truth now, you still wouldn't put your hand inside and tell me you disliked being my prisoner. Think of that before you take me to task, *piccina*! Go now, your father is waiting!'

It simply wasn't fair that he should command her as

if by right, she told herself as she mounted the stairs to her room. Life was unfair! If it weren't, she wouldn't go up in flames every time he looked at her. Not that he cared! And why should he? He had Alessandra, and she had no one, no one at all!

She wouldn't wear the sea-green dress. She told herself it was because she didn't want to, but it was more than that, it was a gesture of independence, to prove to herself that she was still in control of her own life.

Even so, she was more than a little shocked when she saw herself in the looking-glass. No wonder her father had asked what she had been doing with herself to get in such a state! Muddy grass stains marked her coat and her dress, which had been pristine when she had donned it that morning, was crushed and the collar was torn. Standing in front of the glass and looking at herself, she felt hot all over, as she remembered how she had threatened Domenico with the cleaning bill for her clothes. Now all she could think of was the strength of his arms and the wonder of his kisses.

Did she look kissed? She peered at herself. Was that what her father had thought when he had looked at her? What would he think of her? She tried to imagine him kissing Agnes, as she supposed he must do however unbelievable she found it. Indeed her mind boggled at the thought, but at least it was better than dwelling on Domenico's easy mastery of herself.

She flung off her dress, impatient with her own stupidity. She should have known that she wasn't really his prisoner! Yet there had been so many things that she hadn't understood—didn't understand yet! She put on a cream dress with a gold belt and gold chain around the neck, struggling against an inclination to ignore every article that Domenico had bought her in

126

favour of her own discarded jeans and shirt. But why annoy her father? If she wanted answers to the questions she was about to ask him, it was far better to look as much like he thought a woman should as she could. Certainly, in this dress she could have given points to Agnes, she thought. She looked as cool and as crisp as a cucumber, even to the icy look in her eyes. It was quite a transformation scene, seeing she had come in as hot and flustered as a schoolgirl, and she was pleased with the result. She looked more than capable of looking after herself—against all comers, and that included Domenico Manzù! And if she at last felt able to cope with him, why not her father too?

There was no reason that she could see and, as she entered Domenico's study and saw her father's anxious face across the room, she wondered why she had ever worried about holding her own with him.

'Why did you come, Father?' she asked him, smiling as she sat down on one of the leather chairs in front of the fireplace. 'Do you often come to Rome?'

'Not often.' He played with his lips, trying to make up his mind whether he should confide in her or not. 'It was Domenico Manzù's idea that I should come. I asked him to keep an eye on you, and he suggested I should keep an eye on you myself. It's been difficult in the past seeing anything of you, my dear. Agnes——'

'It doesn't matter,' she said, immediately rendered uncomfortable by the mention of his wife's name.

'Because we're too far apart now, although we're father and daughter?' he countered quickly.

'Well, it would be silly to pretend that we've ever been close,' she answered.

'That wasn't the way I wanted it,' he told her. 'These things happen. That's what made me think I would

127

come to Rome—it seemed a good idea for us to spend a few days together. You don't object to that, do you?'

'Of course not!' she hesitated. 'Is that all there is to it, Father?'

'Mostly. I didn't want you to come with things as they are just now. I don't much care for that young man of yours, though I realise I've forfeited the right to say so. If your mother likes him, I suppose there must be more to him than he allowed me to see.'

'Are you talking about Michael Doyle?' Deborah asked.

'Isn't he here with you in Rome?'

'Not exactly,' Deborah said carefully. 'Father, how do you come to know Michael?'

He had the grace to look a little embarrassed. 'Your mother writes to me every now and again, telling me of your doings. She seemed to think Michael Doyle was important to you—shared your artistic interests, that sort of thing! She also told me you were going on holiday with him to Rome. I was worried about you coming here, I have to admit. You may have read in the papers that the son of one of our local managers was kidnapped the other day. We paid up to get him back and he was returned to his parents alive, but it wasn't a pleasant incident. I was afraid something similar might happen to you.'

'You should have told me,' Deborah put in, thinking how casually she had dismissed his warnings when she had gone to see him.

'I didn't want to worry you,' he explained. 'But I didn't think it would do any harm to have a word with your young man——'

'He isn't my young man!'

'He seemed to think he was,' her father said dryly. 'I

got the impression I'd be paying for your wedding before I knew it!'

'Never! Why should you pay?'

'I'm your father——'

'I don't care if you are! I don't want your money!'

'I see,' he said. 'I haven't much else to offer you, Deborah. I work too hard to have much time, and I have other responsibilities.'

'Agnes.'

'And our children.'

Deborah heaved a sigh. 'It isn't because she's your wife that I don't like Agnes. She doesn't like me either!'

'Now there you malign her,' her father said with unexpected humour. 'Agnes only dislikes those she envies or who are much richer than herself.'

Deborah made a face at him. She didn't doubt that Agnes was the complete materialist, but she would have liked to think her stepmother had some reason to envy her the freedom of being young and talented. One day, when she was a sculptor of note, would Agnes envy her then?

'Yes, well, never mind,' she said aloud. 'You summoned Michael to see you?'

'Hardly that,' Mr Beaumont protested. 'I took him out to lunch, if you must know. Not being my daughter, he didn't hesitate to order the most expensive meal on the menu! He also informed me it would be difficult to look after you in Rome as you were doing the whole thing on a shoe-string and if you were tempted to try and cash in by selling some of your work, he could hardly stop you. Everyone would know who you were then, just as everyone at that art college you attended knew you were connected with Beaumont International and had been born with a silver spoon in your mouth.'

Deborah gaped at him. 'But it isn't true! I never told anyone who you were! I didn't want them to know!'

Her father winced. 'These things get about. You'd be surprised!'

'I should! It's true you paid my fees at the College, but that was no wish of mine. How could I get a grant, which was what I wanted to do, when they only allow them to people whose parents earn a lot less than you do?'

'You sound as though you resent my paying for you?'

'Well, so I did! Wouldn't you have done? I want to stand on my own feet!'

Her father looked first sad and then reluctantly amused. 'Signor Manzù said you should have been called Miss Independence!'

Deborah raised her eyebrows. 'He did? When?'

'He telephoned me last night to tell me he had you safe.' Mr Beaumont leaned forward in his chair, his hands lightly clasped together on his knees. Deborah recognised the stance at once. It meant he was about to say something she wouldn't like and that he hoped to hurry over the rough ground of her displeasure as quickly as possible.

'Well?' she prompted him.

'I wasn't satisfied young Doyle understood the danger you might be in——'

'Oh, Father, really! What danger?'

Her father managed to look more sheepish than ever. 'It wasn't just my imagination working overtime,' he rebuked her gently. 'I received a number of anonymous letters, all saying that Beaumont International would be made to pay for their capitalist crimes in the near future, and that neither I nor my family would be safe from

130

their vengeance. Naturally, my first thoughts were for Agnes and the children——'

Naturally! Deborah thought. She was only surprised she had figured at all in her father's calculations, even as an afterthought.

'—but then your mother wrote me about your proposed visit to Rome. I thought I would be able to talk you out of it, but you're every bit as stubborn as she is and you wouldn't listen to anything I said——'

'You didn't say much!' Deborah remembered. 'I thought you were just being difficult.'

'I'm usually thought to be a reasonable man,' Mr Beaumont said drily.

'Perhaps you take the trouble to explain things to other people,' Deborah suggested, almost humbly. 'All you said to me was that you might find yourself harassed if I were recognised as your daughter in Rome. Are you surprised I didn't take you seriously?'

'Maybe I handled you badly——'

'That's just it! You don't have to handle me at all! Do you handle the people you work with? Or do you talk to them as ordinary human beings?'

'They're mostly older than you are, Deborah.'

'I'm twenty-one, Father. Isn't that old enough?'

Mr Beaumont started. 'Twenty-one? I hadn't realised. I suppose one doesn't mark the event in quite the same way as we did in my young days. It's all at eighteen now, isn't it?'

'I don't know. I'm not a great partygoer.' She dismissed the subject with a shrug of her shoulders. There was no point in reminding him that she had seldom received a present from him for any of her birthdays. 'Go on about Michael,' she said. 'Why did you give him a cheque for five hundred pounds?'

'My dear child, you weren't supposed to know about that! Did the young fool tell you about it?'

'I was holding his things just before Domenico's car arrived. The cheque was in a loose envelope and I put it in my pocket——'

Her father frowned. 'He hadn't cashed it? I wonder what the boy was playing at? He couldn't expect to walk into any bank in Rome and cash it, surely?'

'But why give it to him at all?' Deborah asked, as puzzled as her father was as to Michael's actions.

'I wanted him to take you to a hotel,' her father confessed. 'And to see that you didn't go off on your own. I explained to him what was involved and he seemed to understand. He seemed to know all about the spate of kidnappings in Italy and, even if you don't take it seriously, he certainly did! I can't say I liked the fellow, but he seemed bright enough! He told me he had very little money, but that he'd do his best to look after you. Only it would be difficult for him to keep up with you. You have an ample allowance from your mother——'

'I do not!' Deborah was shocked into protest. 'But you *know* I won't accept anything from her now! Not since I left college! I can't live on her for the rest of my life!'

'What do you live on?' her father demanded, equally shocked.

'I worked in the evenings for this holiday. Sometimes I sell a piece of sculpture, but not often. Mostly I do whatever comes my way.' It seemed to Deborah that the whole conversation was getting out of hand. She longed for it to be over, so that she wouldn't have to think about Michael Doyle for a long, long time to come. After this little lot, he was no friend of hers!

132

'I'm going to do a bust of Domenico,' she remembered with a gush of pleasure. 'He says I can choose the marble for it myself!'

Her father was jolted out of his deliberate calm. 'You'd better refuse! My dear girl, have you seen the Manzù collection? You're never going to be able to compete in that class!'

Deborah had had her own doubts about that, but she was not prepared to share them with her father. 'Have you seen my work?' she asked him.

If her father remembered the invitations he had been sent to various showings of the work his daughter had done while attending the art college, he gave no sign of it. 'Your mother says you are very good,' he admitted indulgently. 'But that isn't the same thing as being of the kind of standing that any artist would gain by having a piece included in the Manzù collection!'

'Oh well,' Deborah said easily, 'if Domenico doesn't like it he doesn't have to have it. He might like to have it because I did it—not for its artistic value at all!'

'I doubt that, my dear. It wouldn't do for you to get fond of Signor Manzù,' he added stiffly. 'I know he's been kind to you——'

'*Kind?* He hasn't been kind at all! He's an overbearing brute! He really did kidnap me——'

'Nonsense! I asked him to look out for you. You can't call it kidnapping to invite you to be his house guest in his own palace!'

'What else would you call it? He sent his car to meet me off the airport bus and forced me to accept his hospitality whether I wanted to or not. And Michael was no help at all, if you want to know!'

Her father actually laughed. 'Signor Manzù is a respectable business man—he doesn't have to kidnap anyone to get his own way in a deal. I have the greatest respect for his acumen. If his methods were a little high-handed, I don't think you have much to complain about, my dear. You seem to be on very good terms with him now!'

'Father, don't you *care*——?'

'Now listen to me, Deborah. I have every reason to be grateful to Signor Manzù for looking after you. More than that, he took the trouble to kit you out with some suitable clothes, at my expense it's true, and to show you something of Rome. We are very fortunate to be his guests for a few days. Why, he's even introducing us to some of his closest friends this evening and some of them could be very useful people for me to know. If you want to quarrel with him, you won't do it while I'm on hand to prevent you. I'll send you straight back to England, if I hear you so much as breathe a word against him!'

Deborah faced her father, as stubborn and as angry as he. 'I came to Rome under my own steam and I'll go back the same way! Be as grateful as you like to Signor Domenico Manzù, but I don't owe him a thing!'

'Deborah!'

'No, you listen to me, Father. I refuse to be some pawn on your business board, to be moved here and there at will! I'm responsible for myself and not to anyone else for what I do, and say, and think! If you don't like it, *you* can go back to England!'

She was glad to escape from his society shortly after that. To her surprise her hostess meeting her on her way upstairs invited her to take tea with her. Signora Manzù made her own tea, and drank it with a relish that secretly amused her young guest.

'You have seen the collection?' she said to Deborah.

134

Deborah remembered it with pleasure. 'Yes, I did. How beautiful you are, *signora*! I saw at once where Domenico gets his fine looks!'

The Signora laughed. 'Domenico told me you had recognised me at once,' she said, not without satisfaction. 'You are not shocked, *cara*? It caused a great scandal at the time!'

'You must have thought it was worth it,' Deborah observed. 'And the last word must be yours, *signora*. For as long as the statuette exists, everyone can see your beauty for themselves.'

'Not everyone is as broad-minded as you are,' the Signora said with a small, tight smile.

'But who cares what Alessandra thinks?' Deborah retorted.

The Signora gave her a piercing look. 'You think Domenico doesn't?'

'I don't know,' Deborah admitted, and saw her hostess wilt a little. 'But I'm sure one has to make up one's own mind about these things. I wish I could persuade my father of that!'

Signora Manzù frowned. 'You think he would object to the statuette of me?'

'No. He objects to the things I do, though. I don't like being manipulated! I'm afraid we'll never learn to agree!'

Signora Manzù patted her hand. 'If you will take a word of advice, *cara*, you will find it makes a world of difference who it is who is doing the manipulating. You find it objectionable when it is your father and I find it is so when I think it is Alessandra who is pulling the wires. Shall we make an arrangement between ourselves, you and I? We will support each other in the face of these people and—who knows?—perhaps we

135

shall rid our lives of both of them to a safe distance where we can contemplate them with equanimity? Is it a deal?' She brought out the Americanism with a satisfaction that made Deborah laugh.

'It's a deal,' she agreed, and they solemnly shook hands like two conspirators.

Deborah could have done with her new partner beside her when she came face to face with Domenico in the hall on her way back to her own room.

He lifted his eyebrows at the sight of her. 'I hope you managed to reassure your father?' he inquired with less than his usual tact.

Deborah, who scarcely ever lost her temper, did so now. She had come through a trying few hours and she thought she had acquitted herself well—*no thanks to him!*

'How much did he pay *you*?' she threw at him. 'Enough to make it worth your while, I suppose, or you would have left me to my own devices! Which I would very much have preferred, let me tell you! How dared you frighten the life out of me——'

'When did I do that?' His eyes laughed into hers. 'You weren't scared at all, *piccina*!'

'Of course I was scared! I'd never seen you before and I knew nothing about you! How was I to know what evil you intended doing me?'

He put his head on one side. 'A little excitement is not the same as being afraid,' he mocked her. 'You knew all the time I wouldn't hurt you. Come, confess it, Deborah! You were more curious than fearful, were you not?'

Deborah had no intention of doing anything of the sort. 'You took advantage of me!'

He looked up heavenwards. 'Where is the Mouth of

136

Truth now? You would get your fingers nipped for that, *cara mia*!'

'I would not!' she flung back at him. 'I feel nothing but contempt for you that you'd accept my father's money——'

His fingers bit into her arm, causing her to cry out, but he paid no attention to her distress. On a rising tide of panic she saw that he was now every bit as angry as she. He dragged her into the study, where she had so recently been talking to her father, and slammed the door behind them.

'What makes you think I would accept a penny from your father?' he demanded, his face no more than a few inches from her own.

'Why would you have kidnapped me otherwise?' Her eyes misted and she would have liked to have looked away, but he held her so tightly she could not. 'Michael was paid five hundred pounds to nanny me while I was in Rome—how much were you paid?'

'Not one lira!'

'I don't believe you! Why else should you go to so much trouble——'

'Very reluctantly, to begin with,' he told her. 'I don't usually waste time on the daughters of my business acquaintances, but your father asked only that I should make sure you came to no harm while you were in Italy and I could scarcely refuse such a request.'

'You didn't have to keep me a prisoner in your home!'

'That was my pleasure,' he said, with a slow, sardonic smile. 'I liked the thought of you being my prisoner.'

What Deborah would have said, she never knew, for the telephone bell rang insistently beside them. Without letting her go, Domenico reached out a hand across the desk and picked up the receiver. Deborah listened to the flood of Italian that was exchanged between him and the unseen woman at the other end of the line.

'*Bene*, Flavia,' he said at last. '*Viene ad un cocktail questa sera?*'

Deborah couldn't tell whether his invitation had been refused or accepted. 'Who is Flavia?' she asked as he put the receiver back on its cradle. 'Isn't Alessandra enough for you?'

'Do you object to my having other girl-friends on her behalf, or on your own?'

The question slowly permeated Deborah's consciousness, followed by a wave of humiliation that he should ask her such a thing. 'You can keep a whole harem for all I care!' she retorted briskly.

'Alessandra wouldn't care for that at all,' he drawled, his eyes narrowing as he looked at her. 'And nor would Flavia. That leaves only you, Deborah Beaumont. What ideas you do have, *piccolina*! *Dio mio*, but you tempt me to make you tonight's favourite. You would not say no to me for long!'

'For long enough!' Deborah declared, but she didn't believe it herself, so why should he?

CHAPTER NINE

'My dear little Deborah, deceive yourself if you must, but you don't deceive me!' There was a distinct gleam in his eyes that unsettled her.

138

'I don't know what you're talking about!' she denied. She tried to rid herself of the tight constriction in her throat. 'I'm not your prisoner now that my father is here, so you can't force me to anything!'

'Bravely said!' he admired.

'Can you?' she insisted.

The pressure of his fingers on the small of her back set her heart thumping against her ribs. 'Shall we find out?' he whispered against her cheek.

'No!' She was overtaken by panic.

'No? Then confess that you would like me to and I'll set you free!'

'I won't be bullied!' she snapped.

'Of course not,' he said at once. 'I'm only asking you to tell me the truth, that you are not the indifferent English rose you have been busy pretending to be.'

'And how will that help?' she sighed.

'It would be a beginning, Deborah. I'm not asking more than that for now.'

'But a beginning of *what*? Alessandra——'

'Forget Alessandra! This is between you and me. Well, Deborah?'

'You have behaved abominably!' she berated him. 'For all you knew I might have been scared out of my wits, thinking I'd been kidnapped and—and so on!'

'And so on?' he taunted her.

'No girl would have felt safe——'

'Did you suppose I would seduce you while you were under the same roof as my mother and sister?'

She opened her eyes wide. 'How am I to know what you're capable of? I wasn't to know that you were only acting as my father's lackey! You might have had any number of reasons for kidnapping me!'

His hands tightened on her back. 'I am not and never

139

have been your father's lackey!'

'No?' she retorted, glad to have found a stick to beat him with. 'Then why did you keep me here? I was quite all right with my friends!'

'Perhaps I don't approve of your independent ways any more than your father does,' he said quietly. 'It was time you grew up, Deborah Beaumont, and became a woman, and you were not going to do that junketing around with your friends. You would have found yourself in time, I have no doubt, but I wasn't prepared to wait. England can be as far away as the moon if you are a busy man with as many commitments as I have. Do you understand now?'

'I suppose I do, but there doesn't seem to be much future in it. You see, I won't—I *can't*——' She broke off, aware of the impossibility of explaining to him that she couldn't see her way to becoming his mistress when he had yet to ask her to enter into any kind of relationship with him.

'You underrate yourself!' he said dryly. 'Don't you know how much I want you, my love?'

She shook her head. 'It wouldn't do! I hate to sound like Alessandra, but you have your family to consider——'

'I thought you liked my family?' he protested.

'*I do!*'

He frowned. 'I agree there will be difficulties, but nothing that can't be overcome. Is the Roman nobility such a frightening proposition to you?'

'Of course not!' She smiled a rather wavery smile. 'Where ignorance is bliss, I suppose! You see, I don't know much about it. Only that you attend the papal court sometimes——'

'On increasingly rare occasions. There used to be a

great deal of protocol involved, but nowadays most of the old rituals have been cleared away—and a good thing too!'

'But there are some occasions when you still attend the Pope, and I shouldn't like to be hidden away from him as though you were ashamed of me—and you would be obliged to leave me behind, wouldn't you?'

'In the beginning,' he agreed. 'I admit I hope you will one day want to join me in the practice of my faith——'

She winced. 'What have the rituals of the black nobility to do with that?' she demanded.

'Very little,' he admitted carefully. 'One likes to do what one's ancestors have always done, but'—and he smiled at her, causing her heart to lurch within her— 'I would willingly give up those few minutes of glory for you!'

'But your family will suffer!' she sighed.

'My mother has never enjoyed such displays,' he reassured her. 'She feels that even today women are not precisely welcome in the Vatican. She will be on your side, *amante*, it is I who will be the one to suffer her displeasure if I leave you alone too often!'

She thought he was joking. 'I don't believe your mother is as unconventional as you want me to think. She may not feel the same as Alessandra about her faith, but I'm sure her sense of tradition is equally great. She wouldn't approve at all of your giving up any of it for me.'

'You think not? I have always found her a great one for compromise and I had hoped you were the same. You haven't anything against my faith, have you?'

Deborah dismissed that as lightly as she felt it deserved. 'Of course not! But this isn't a question of faith,

141

is it? This is a family matter. How could you go on as before if you were breaking all the rules! I wouldn't feel good enough for you like that, and my pride wouldn't let you hide me away either, so how could we possibly be happy?'

'Could you ever be happy away from me?' he countered.

He was very sure of his ground. She could feel it in the caress of his fingers against her back and could see it in the confident set of his head.

'I was happy enough before I ever met you,' she said.

His air of command was very hard to withstand. 'You're a different person now,' he said in her ear. 'You've grown up, little one, like a single lovely rose coming into bloom. Could you bloom like that for any other man?'

She shrugged her shoulders, knowing in her heart that he was right. 'A few clothes!' she scoffed. '*And* paid for by my father! I'm still the same me inside them.'

'They're not paid for yet,' he reminded her. 'And I did quite well with you before I took you shopping, I seem to remember. If I were to kiss you again, you would not go on denying you were made for me, I am thinking!'

Deborah clenched her fists against his chest. 'That isn't kind! Domenico, I have to go away from you! Surely you see that?'

He let her go so suddenly that she was afraid her knees might give way under her and she sat down quickly on the nearest chair. He had his back to her and she couldn't see what he was thinking. How could she bear to go away and never see him again?

'What about the bust you are going to do of me?'

his voice broke across her thoughts. 'Won't you need to see me for that?'

'I'll send it to you——'

'You will not! You will sculpt it here in the palace or not at all! Well, *piccolina*, which is it to be?'

'That isn't fair!' she exclaimed.

'No, it isn't,' he agreed promptly. 'Haven't you a saying in England that all is fair in love and war? If you won't stay with me of your own free will, this is both!' He took a step towards her chair, standing over her, his eyes narrowed as he surveyed her. 'Shall we go and choose the marble together tomorrow?'

She nodded her head, glad he had taken the decision out of her hands for the moment at least. She looked up at him, her eyes bright with unshed tears. 'When I've finished it you'll have to allow me to give it to you!'

He was keeping his temper on a very short leash and she was more than a little afraid that she had pressed him too far.

'I think it better we should decide our relationship on a day-to-day basis,' he said at last. 'Tonight you will attend my party as your father's daughter and meet my friends. Tomorrow, I shall take you to the quarry to choose the marble. The day after—who knows? But the day after that, my darling, you will have to make up your mind to end the battle between us. If you won't come to me willingly, then it will have to be unwillingly, but come to me you will!' He bent his head close to hers. 'You will not be unwilling for long, I promise you that!'

His kiss was angry and demanding and, when she tried to pull away, his arms closed about her, holding her a prisoner against the hard frame of his body and

143

the excitement that she always felt when she was close to him flared into life, kindling her own desires with a sure touch.

'Domenico,' she began. 'I can't think when you—— Please, won't you be gentle with me——'

'Then, by God, you'd better come willingly, for I mean to have you one way or the other. You have my word on that!'

He kissed her again, but the anger had gone out of him and she felt his tenderness like a living flame between them, warming her and building up the fires of her passion until she could think of nothing and no one but him and of the love she bore him.

When he lifted his head she felt only a sense of loss. 'The day after tomorrow, my sweet, can't come quickly enough for me,' he said, 'but you'd better go now and get ready for the party. I may forget my promise to you otherwise!'

Deborah went in a daze, filled with a mad hope that he would keep his word and would find some way to keep her with him, but halfway up the stairs common sense prevailed and she knew she would have to leave both Italy and him long before then. If she couldn't be his wife, then there was nothing else for her to do but go, even though it should break her heart. She was sufficiently her mother's daughter to want all or nothing—but, dear God, she hoped she would be strong enough to bear the desolation that would go with her.

Dressed in one of her brand new dresses, she felt a stranger to herself on her father's arm. She had thought it was to be a fairly small party, but the palace was already crowded with people and although she had been faithfully introduced to every one of them she had no idea who the half of them were. All she had been aware of was the naked curiosity with which they had greeted her, coupled with an unexpected desire to please her that had bewildered her father almost as much as it had herself.

'Do you suppose they think I'm somebody else?' she whispered to him.

Her father surveyed the crowded room with satisfaction. 'Beaumont's must be more important in Italy than I'd thought. I'm glad you came after all, my dear. I always knew Domenico Manzù was a useful contact, but he's certainly coming up trumps this evening.'

'I don't think that's why Domenico gave the party,' Deborah put in, disliking the idea with a violence that could only dismay her.

'Why else?' her father grunted. 'He would hardly have given it for you, now would he?'

'He might,' she said.

Her father looked quite shocked and then thoughtful. 'Are you getting sweet on him?' he asked with his customary lack of tact. 'Because there's nothing for you there, my dear. His family will see to that! These old European families are far more sticky than our own aristocracy and when it comes to marriage they never look outside their own ranks. They're unbelievably jealous of all their old traditions. I suppose it comes of living in a republic where no new nobles can be created.'

Deborah said nothing. She had known it all for herself, of course, but she found it all the more lowering to hear her father confirm her worst fears. It made Alessandra seem a more suitable wife than ever. With relief she turned away from her father to Gianetta, looking suddenly beautiful on the arm of her fiancé.

'Where *is* Alessandra?' she hissed at her.

Gianetta shrugged. 'Who cares?'

Her brother frowned at her. '*Ha mal di testa!*' he said with quelling emphasis.

'So she says she has a headache,' Gianetta translated indifferently. 'I think she's taken flight because you've never put on a party like this for *her*!'

Deborah's conscience smote her. 'I hope she's not staying away because of me. I think she knows I don't like her very much and perhaps she thinks it will spoil the evening for me——' She became conscious of the Manzùs staring at her in mocking astonishment and tried a new tack. 'It's a splendid party! It was very kind of you both and your mother to hold it while my father and I are here.'

'Kind?' Gianetta queried faintly. 'But——'

Her brother stopped her with a look. 'Do you like my friends?' he asked Deborah. 'Have they made you feel welcome?'

Her eyes fell. 'Very,' she admitted. 'Perhaps every European feels at home in Rome because it belongs to all of us—a little bit?'

'Hmm,' he said, and smiled. 'I'm glad you feel at home anyway.' He looked round the room. 'Have you decided where your bust of me should stand?' he asked her.

She shook her head, feeling unaccountably shy of him. 'Wouldn't that be rather impertinent of me?' she countered.

'On the contrary, I hope it will be the first of many such decisions!'

Deborah's hand sought a firmer hold on her father's arm. She felt his muscles stiffen against her touch and she took a quick step away from him, trying to pretend to herself it was no more than she had expected. At the same moment there was one of those silences that sometimes come over a group of people as Alessandra made her entrance, looking for all the world like an Italian version of Queen Victoria.

Gianetta made a face and called across the room to her. '*Hai ancora mal di testa*, Alessandra?'

'It is not well,' Alessandra returned civilly, making her way across the room towards them, 'but I knew it was my duty to come to help Domenico's mother with all these people.' She twitched her shoulders angrily. 'He has no consideration—as if such a party couldn't wait for another few days when she wouldn't have house-guests to contend with as well!'

Gianetta's previous pleasure and beauty fell from her, leaving her white and angry. A storm of Italian left her lips, refusing to be stilled even by her fiancé's pleas. Deborah could understand very little of it, but even she could make out the last cutting sentence. 'I am here to stand beside my mother as Domenico's hostess, Sandra. It's not at all necessary for you to make yourself ill minding our business for us!'

'I know how you feel, *cara* Gianetta,' Alessandra said calmly. 'Nevertheless, we all have to remember that you will not be available for such social duties for much longer. You have chosen another way of life, haven't you? But we shall manage very well without you. *I* have never been one to shrink from doing my duty, I can promise you.'

Domenico, with a sidelong glance at his sister's furious face, put his hand on Alessandra's arm and drew her away. 'Aren't you being rather previous, Sandra?' he murmured. 'I don't recollect ever inviting you to act as my hostess and, besides, I thought you knew, my mother and I are giving this party *for* our

147

house-guests to introduce them to our friends in Rome.'

Deborah stood frozen to the ground. Much as she disliked the Italian girl, she couldn't help feeling for her even if she had asked for the humiliating snub Domenico had given her.

'Poor Alessandra!' she said.

'*Poor!*' Gianetta exclaimed with contempt. 'How can you say so? I have never disliked anyone more! I don't know what I shall do if Domenico marries her! And she's always the same! Even when she's telling you how welcome you are, you know she's wishing you would drop dead. When I think of the times she's gone behind my back dripping her poison to all our friends, I wish I never had to speak to her again!'

Deborah uttered a low laugh of sympathy. 'I know someone else just like that! She always pretends she can't quite remember my name——' Belatedly, she remembered her father standing beside her and broke off, confused and guilty. She could have been referring to anyone, of course, but it was too late to go on now. He would know that she had been talking about Agnes! She sent him a wordless look of apology, but he refused to accept it. His mouth tightened into an angry line.

'Any trouble between you and Agnes has always been of your own making,' he told her bleakly. 'You would never accept that she and I had any right to be happy together!'

Deborah bit her lip. 'Not now, Father,' she begged him.

'I blame your mother,' he went on regardless.

'*Not now!*' Deborah said again.

Her father sighed. 'It's never the right time in your opinion for us to talk together. Just like your mother—

148

burying your head in the sand! Only with her it was always my work she took exception to. Seemed to think money grew on trees and that I could spend all my time with her!'

'Instead of with Agnes?' Deborah said sweetly, and then wished she hadn't. 'Oh, what does it matter? I wasn't talking about Agnes anyway!'

'Agnes is my wife——'

It was Gianetta who succeeded in diverting his attention. She smiled at him in a way that could only concentrate his attention on herself and edged him away from Deborah a few inches at a time. 'There is someone over there Domenico particularly wants you to meet,' she challenged him. 'He is a very clever business man also and is full of ideas about how Beaumont's could expand into the Common Market countries.'

Mr Beaumont followed his young hostess like a lamb, his good humour completely restored. Deborah's lips trembled into a laugh. 'Has the poor man ever heard of Beaumont's, do you think?' she wondered aloud.

Cesare followed his fiancée's progress with an amused look. 'I doubt it,' he said, 'but he will do anything for Gianetta. He has only to listen and your father will do the talking, no?'

'Yes,' said Deborah. 'His business is his whole life.'

'But not yours,' Cesare said quickly. 'We must live and let live. His life has not been yours for many years now. We all understand that, *signorina*. Domenico has told us you are a great artist and not in the business world at all!'

But Deborah feared the damage had been done. Her father would not forget her disparaging reference to

149

Agnes easily, and he had never been one to leave a painful subject alone. It augured badly for their planned outing the next day, she thought, and wondered how she could best persuade him that Agnes was better left behind in England for the next few days. They would never get to understand each other better while the ghost of his second wife stalked through their every conversation together.

It was not Agnes, however, but Beaumont's that caused the row between them the next day. Deborah's father disliked sightseeing at the best of times and when he found he was expected to visit a whole lot of ancient churches in his daughter's company, he would only go on the understanding that she would listen carefully to what he had come to Rome to tell her.

'Visiting churches is more in your mother's line. She has more time for that sort of thing,' he muttered as they boarded a bus for the Via Veneto, the most famous street in Rome.

'It won't do you any harm,' Deborah retorted heart-lessly. 'We can always go on to the catacombs if you like?'

'If we have to,' her father agreed. 'But you'll listen to me first, Deborah! That's understood, isn't it?'

'Yes, that's understood,' she sighed. 'Shall we have a cup of coffee at one of the cafés?'

'Very well,' he consented. But it was not easy to find a café that would allow them to sit out on the pavement when they were expecting rain. Deborah was all for going inside, but her father was afraid of being overheard. He looked completely out of place in the fashionable street, clutching his rolled umbrella to him and with the buttons of his coat straining across his thickening waistline.

'Deborah, I've been thinking,' he said, sinking heavily on to a rain-damp chair. 'I was talking to Signora Manzù last night and you seem to have made a very good impression there—can't think how, considering what you were wearing when she first saw you! She could well have thought you were one of these dreadful hippies, or whatever they're calling themselves these days! But at least your mother always had good manners and she seems to have passed them on to you when you care to make use of them. I think you're on to a good thing here, my dear. If you play your cards well, the Manzùs may accept you as a possible partner for Domenico. The Signora was very impressed when I told her the dowry I was thinking of settling on you on the day of your marriage. Daresay it was rather better than anything Alessandra's parents are likely to come up with!'

Deborah clenched her teeth. 'I don't want a dowry,' she said.

'No, well, I can't say I shall like coughing up such a sum for you much,' her father went on. 'But it will be worth it if I can get Domenico Manzù for a son-in-law. The next time I come to Rome it may be to open our branch of Beaumont's International here in Rome! What do you think of that?'

'I don't think Domenico is interested in Beaumont's,' Deborah answered with deliberate restraint.

'He will be!'

Deborah blenched. 'But I don't think of Domenico like that, Father! Everyone knows he plans to marry Alessandra.'

'Perhaps he did, one can't tell with these foreigners, but I think you'll find his mother will soon change his mind for him. An admirable woman! Understood im-

151

mediately what I was talking about and wasn't afraid to say so. She didn't admit the Manzùs were less wealthy than they were once, but it was as plain as daylight that she would welcome having Beaumont's substance behind her. No, you listen to me, Deborah,' he went on as his daughter made to interrupt him. 'You could do a lot worse for yourself than ally yourself with young Domenico Manzù!'

'Father, I'm not a business asset to be bought and sold by you or anyone else! As soon as I can arrange it, I shall move out of the Palazzo Manzù and rejoin my friends in their borrowed apartment——'

'And turn your back on the best bit of good fortune ever to come your way? You wouldn't be such a fool! I know you take after your mother, but you have my blood in your veins as well as hers! This time, my dear, you'll do as you're told or that will be the last you hear from me! If you turn down Domenico Manzù, I'll have nothing more to do with you, no matter what sort of a mess you succeed in making of your life!'

Deborah squinted at him over her coffee cup. She felt cold inside, cold with a despair as sharp as any knife. She felt as though her life was bleeding away inside her and that the cold she felt was a foretaste of a life lived without any emotion at all—a life without Domenico!

'Is that a promise?' she asked in a futile attempt at a joke.

'Deborah——'

'Because I hope you weren't serious,' she hurried on, 'as Domenico is the last person in the world I'd marry! I'm afraid Beaumont's will have to do without my cooperation after all, but it's managed without me all these years, so I expect it'll get along without this splendid Italian connection. As for me, I'll see you around some time, Father. Remember me to Agnes when you see her.' She stood up, taking a last sip of coffee in the hopes that it would warm her a little. Perhaps she had caught a chill. 'Don't forget you owe Domenico for my clothes! I'm sorry they won't fit Agnes, but I expect you'll be able to realise something on them if you try hard enough. Goodbye, Father.'

He stood up also. 'Goodbye? But where are you going?'

'Anywhere. I'm going anywhere where I can be by myself and have nothing whatever to do with Beaumont International——'

'But what shall I tell the Manzùs?'

There was something rather pathetic about the agonised, hurt look with which he regarded her, as if he couldn't understand what he had done to upset her. It made her feel quite maternal towards him.

'Don't worry, Father,' she said. 'They'll understand that you did your best to keep me on the straight and narrow business path! I won't be any loss to any of them.'

Her father frowned. 'I thought you were in love with Domenico——'

Deborah forced a smile. 'I thought so too. Funny, I don't feel anything now. All I want is never to have to see him again!' She was surprised to find that she was crying. 'Oh, Father!' she wept. 'He'll think that's why I came to Rome—just to trap him into marriage on your say-so!'

'Now why should he think that?' Mr Beaumont asked awkwardly.

'Why? How could he think otherwise? He'll think I'm as bad as Alessandra! She thinks of nothing but

153

her wretched family name, and he'll think that I think of nothing but the family firm! That I'd even sacrifice myself for it, as Alessandra would on her particular altar! I've never felt so *cheap* and despicable in my whole life!'

'But there's nothing wrong with you taking an interest in your father's firm. You're making too much of this, my dear. Now, come on, dry your tears and we'll say no more about it. We'll go and look at those churches of yours and you can tell me all about them. How's that?'

Deborah's face crumpled and her shoulders shook. 'I don't want to go! I want to be by myself! We're both fools, Father, only I'm a bigger one than you are! Domenico doesn't want to marry me—he wants me as his mistress! And I wanted to accept, if you want to know! I may have done if you hadn't tried to sell me to him as part of a business deal. All those clothes! And I let him buy them! No wonder he thought I was making unnecessary difficulties when he said he might have to leave me behind sometimes when he went to the Vatican—he probably thought I was already bought and paid for too! Well, you can tell him from me that I want nothing from either of you! I'm going back to my friends!'

She turned on her heel and left him where she stood, not daring to cross the road, blinded as she was by tears, but running up the pavement all the way to the Pincine Gate. Then, when she looked back, she couldn't see her father at all. For the first time since her arrival she was alone in Rome.

CHAPTER TEN

SHE had been walking aimlessly through the park for some time before she realised that she didn't have the address of the apartment where her friends were staying. She had left it behind in the pocket of the coat she had arrived in. Vainly, she tried to remember what it had been, but being in a foreign language it was all the more difficult to summon up the strange words. Nevertheless, she decided, she was not going back to the Palazzo Manzù. Nothing, but nothing, would induce her to set foot on Domenico's property ever again!

It was raining by the time she reached the Villa Borghese where the buses were lined up ready to take their quota of tourists on their afternoon tours of the different parts of Rome. Someone asked her if she had a ticket and which language she spoke, and although she had no ticket one was pressed into her hand and she was hurried on to the nearest coach with a great many Japanese and a handful of Americans. She allowed herself to be pushed down towards the back, reflecting that at least she would be out of the rain for the greater part of the afternoon.

The girl who sat down next to her announced that she had been born in Holland, was an American citizen, and had just finished doing a tour of duty with the American diplomatic service in Central Africa. 'I shall be going home soon,' she added, leaving Deborah to wonder if she meant by that America or Holland.

It was hard to make her mind a blank and to go

along with the herd, but thanks to her chatty neighbour, Deborah almost succeeded. They went first to the church of Santa Maria Maggiore, decorated with the first gold to be brought back from South America as the gift of Queen Isabella of Spain. Here they peered at the celebrated relics of the manger where Christ was reputed to have been placed after His birth in Bethlehem. Deborah willed herself to feel some of the proper sentiments, but what with the Confessional being completely dominated by an enormous statue of Pope Pius IX, coupled with her own misery at what Domenico must be thinking of her, she might have well been looking at any bit of old timber and she was annoyed with herself for being so unromantic about something that had been treasured in Rome for many hundreds of years.

In the church of St Peter in Chains, she felt much the same about Moses, one of Michelangelo's acknowledged masterpieces. She put a coin in the machinery that operated the light that spotlit the statue and stared gloomily at the marvellously veined hands and the horns of light on his head. She wished Michael were with her, for he would have put the piece in the history of its time for her and she might have appreciated it better. As it was, it only served to remind her that she was unlikely now to complete the bust she had been going to do of Domenico.

By the time her group had trooped in and out of St John in Laterum, billed as the Cathedral Church of Rome and the world, Deborah was beginning to worry as to what she was going to do next. She had little money with her and only the clothes she stood up in and, if she didn't remember the address she had been given soon, she had absolutely nowhere to go. She barely glanced through the rain at the Holy Staircase that tradition has it Jesus climbed up to the first floor of Pontius Pilate's house in Jerusalem. Instead, she settled back into her seat and gave herself up to misery.

Their guide announced they were now on their way to the catacombs and the Dutch-American girl beside her made an enthusiastic noise of assent.

'I suppose you have seen them before?' she said to Deborah.

'No, why should you think that?' Deborah asked, startled.

'You have an air about you, as though you had lived in Rome for a long, long time,' the other girl said. 'You look completely at home here—not a stranger like the rest of us.'

'Do I?' Deborah was plainly astonished. 'I've only been here a few days, but I do feel at home here. I'd like to live here always.'

The American girl shrugged. 'Why don't you?'

'How?'

The American laughed. 'Marry a Roman! That's how I became an American, though it didn't last very long. He was killed in Vietnam, and I didn't get along with his folks, so I took a job travelling about the world. If I see anywhere I want to live more than America, I shall look around for a native and grab him! It worked very well the first time round, so why not again?'

Deborah found herself laughing. 'I wish it were so simple!'

'But it is!' the American insisted. 'Choose the most likely man for you and ask him to teach you a few words of Italian—and pouf! it's done!'

Deborah tried to imagine herself asking Domenico to teach her to speak Italian, but she could not. The cold misery that had been with her ever since she had started out with her father settled in again round her heart and she could have cried out with the pain of it.

The rain was pouring down by the time they left the city by the gate of St Sebastian, formerly the Porta Appia. The Arch of Drusus stood in splendid desolation guarding the way on to what must be one of the most famous roads in the world. The coach paused by the chapel that marked the traditional site of St Peter's meeting with his Lord as he left Rome to escape the worst of the persecutions of the Christians by Nero. '*Domine, quo vadis?*' (Master, where are you going?) he asked. And the other replied, 'I go to Rome to be crucified a second time.' Overcome, Peter returned to Rome, to be crucified as his Master had been before him, with only this difference, that Peter was crucified upside down.

The Appian Way showed signs of its age. The coach rattled over the ancient cobbles and came to a stop outside the Catacombs of Domitilla.

'Here you will have a guide from the Redemptorist Fathers,' their own guide told them. 'The catacombs are the property of the Vatican and we, Roman guides, are not permitted to take visitors inside what is technically foreign territory.'

They walked through some pretty gardens in the rain, making a mad dash for the entrance. With their tickets clutched in their hands, they were herded down a flight of concrete steps and came out in an underground basilica where their priest-guide was waiting for them. He was very young and fair, and his heavily accented Germanic English was difficult to understand and only a fear of getting lost in the eleven miles of underground passages made Deborah hurry to keep up

158

with the busload of tourists as they snaked their way through the burrows where the early Christians had first buried their dead.

A musty, warm, damp smell pervaded the passages. The flat, horizontal graves on either side were black and mysterious. The larger ones had been used by whole families, but there were others, much smaller, where the pathetic bodies of tiny children had been carefully placed. There were frescoes too, here and there, most of them with Christian motifs still instantly recognisable as being the same as those in use today in the Catholic and Orthodox churches of both the Eastern and Western traditions.

Deborah, already last in the queue, hung back for a moment to take a closer look at a fish carved into a piece of marble that had been let into the wall. Near it was the tomb of a carpenter, the tools of his trade represented beside his name to show what manner of work he had done in this life. A little further on was the tomb of an undertaker, and then a whole lot of vacant black spaces whose occupiers had long since fallen back into dust and complete anonymity.

She felt a hand reach out for her wrist and nearly fell apart herself with fright. 'Let me go!' she ordered fiercely.

'Hey, it's us!' Mary's blessedly familiar voice greeted her. 'Are you doing the same tour? We didn't see you on the coach.'

'I didn't see you either!' Deborah gasped.

John, never very far away from Mary, grinned his schoolboy smile. 'How are you getting on?' he asked.

'I've run away,' Deborah confessed. 'I can't tell you how glad I am to see you both! I forgot to bring your address with me and I was feeling absolutely desperate because I *can't* go back! It was awful—and my father came——'

'You look beautiful!' said Mary. 'I do like your hair that way! Wait till Patty sees it! She'll be pea-green——'

'Michael isn't with us any longer!' John cut her off.

Deborah's eyes widened. 'Why not?'

John looked uncomfortable. 'Well, you weren't there and I guess we didn't get along too well together. We didn't push him out exactly, but neither did we stop him when he suggested it. He always was the fifth wheel on the coach, wasn't he?'

'Was he?' Deborah didn't know any longer what he had been. 'Does that mean you'd rather I didn't——'

'Of course not!' Mary's voice was as warm and sincere as ever. 'We've missed you being round, to tell the truth. Even Patty and Jerry, who never notice anything except themselves, were wishing you were with us yesterday. They'd seen the most gorgeous statue and wanted to know your opinion of it!'

'They should have asked Michael,' Deborah suggested. 'He could have told them exactly.'

'*Michael?*' her friends exclaimed in unison. Then John added, 'We've never liked to say before, Debbie, but he doesn't know nearly as much as he pretends he does. If you ask me, you're better off without him. You'd never have done anything great of your own while you let him hang around feeding off your talent.'

Deborah supposed she should have been used to her friends' plain speaking by now, but the fact of the matter was that she wasn't.

'I always thought you liked Michael?' she said.

'No, honey, we *liked* you! We put up with Michael. At least, John and I did, Patty and Jerry used to spike his guns whenever they could for the fun of it. Now, tell us what's been happening to you? I suppose your father arranged for you to be whisked away like that? You have to hand it to him, he certainly chose the right place in Rome for you to go! Is the Manzù collection as fabulous as everyone says it is?'

'More!' Deborah told her. The knowledge that a bust by her would now never be part of it was like a physical pain inside her and some of what she was feeling must have shown on her face, for John put a comforting hand on her shoulder and gave her a push down the narrow passage to where they could hear the young priest still talking away to the group.

'We'd better catch them up or we may get lost down here for ever.' he advised. 'Are you coming back with us now, Debbie?'

Deborah nodded. 'I'll have to borrow a nightie——' she began.

'Not necessary,' Mary gurgled into laughter. 'Have you forgotten that we still have your suitcase?'

It was like another life, Deborah thought, and her time at the Manzù palace might never have been. Perhaps she had dreamed the whole adventure—but no, she knew she had not. Her imagination would never have been the equal of the reality of being held in Domenico's arms and of being kissed by him. Would he be glad to be rid of her? In the end he would be, but she thought he might miss her a little at first——

They almost ran into the people ahead of them and Deborah caught a glimpse of Patty's and Jerry's eager faces as they listened to the almost incomprehensible accents of the priest.

'And now I tell ze joke,' he said.

But Deborah never heard what it was that made the

listening group break into polite laughter. Supposing she never saw Domenico again? Would she read in the newspaper one day of his marriage to Alessandra and go on living just as though nothing had happened? She didn't know if she could. Her body cried out for the sight and sound of him every moment she was away from him. It had not been like that with Michael, even though she had once thought that she had been in love with him. She hadn't really missed him at all in the last few days. Indeed, it had been rather pleasant to be without him and not to have to concern herself with his endless complaints about the quality of their way of life. She tried to dwell on the good times they had shared together, but all she could bring to mind was Michael telling her to pay for his meals with hers at the canteen; Michael slaying her pride in the work she had done at the art college they had both attended; Michael's bitterness at the smallness of the grants they were expected to live on and his jealousy of the small luxuries her mother had managed to provide for her only daughter.

'People like your mother will never admit it, but it's we artists who give them life!' he had burst out one day. 'So what if they prefer their suburban lives, their brightest hours spent glued to a television set? It's our function to blight their contentment, to make them see what the real world is like!'

She was glad now that she no longer had to look at the world through Michael's eyes—or her father's either. Both saw only what they wanted to see, one reducing everything to nothing and the other everything to money. She had glimpsed a new world, shot through with glory—Domenico's world!

'Come on, we'd better go,' John's voice cut across

her thoughts. 'What's the betting that it's still raining?'

Mary smiled affectionately at him. 'Does it matter?'

'Not as long as we're together!' he smiled back at her.

It was raining. The group lingered by the little shop beside the entrance for as long as they could, but in the end they had to dash back to the coaches in the same manner they had made their entrance, splashing through the puddles as they went.

'We'll take our respective coaches back to the Via Veneto,' Mary suggested. 'We'll see you there!'

But Deborah hesitated, still unsure of her welcome. 'Are you sure Patty and Jerry won't mind?'

'Don't be silly!'

Deborah blinked, a little of the cold despair round her heart making room for a warm gratitude to her friends. 'Thank you,' she said. 'And thank you too for not asking questions. I will tell you all about it, but not yet.'

Mary only laughed at her. 'You don't have to tell us anything you don't want to,' she assured her. 'And don't worry about Patty and Jerry—they won't ask you anything either.' She grinned cheerfully, running her tongue round her lips in a cheeky gesture. 'With any luck they won't notice you've returned to the fold! You know what they are!'

Somewhat comforted, Deborah got back on her own coach and suggested that the American girl should take a turn beside the window. 'Not that you can see anything because the windows steam up as soon as everyone sits down.'

'I saw you with your friends,' the American told her. 'There was someone else looking at you too from the front of the party. Did you see him?'

Deborah shook her head. 'What was he like?'

'We-ell, perhaps he didn't know you but just thought he'd like to! He looked pretty seedy, now I come to think about it, not at all like your other friends.'

Deborah merely smiled. Could it have been Michael? Fervently, she hoped not! And yet how strange it was for her not to want to see Michael. Could she really have changed so dramatically in a couple of days? But yes, she thought she had. The transformation had been as great as the change of a caterpillar into a butterfly—and it had all been Domenico's doing. Perhaps she had had more in common with Galatea than she had thought, only being brought to life was such a painful business, she thought she might have preferred to be left as a lifeless statue all her days.

It had stopped raining when they arrived at the Via Veneto. She rejoined her friends and they set out to walk the short distance to the apartment where they were staying.

'Don't expect too much,' Patty warned Deborah. 'It's a couple of rooms, not a palace, you know!'

Deborah knew it was only a figure of speech, but it hurt all the same. 'I wasn't expecting a palace,' she said.

'That's all right, then,' Patty confirmed. 'But you have been staying in one, haven't you?'

'Yes,' Deborah admitted. But such was the look on her face that not even Patty persisted with any further references to where she had been for the last few days. Instead she cast a speaking look at Jerry and, with a slight shrug of her shoulders, said, 'We got rid of Michael. You don't mind, do you?'

'Why should I?' Deborah murmured.

'Well, *you* should know!'

Deborah quickened her pace, not even trying to take in which way they were going. 'Michael helped me with my work,' she said stiffly, 'but I don't have to be with him all the time!'

Patty stared at her, and even Mary raised her eyebrows in friendly disbelief. 'You've changed your tune!' Jerry said frankly. 'We all thought that where you're concerned, the sun rose and set between Michael's shoulder-blades. You were forever quoting his opinions at us!'

'Then I apologise,' Deborah retorted on the edge of anger. 'But it would be all the same to me if I never saw Michael again!'

'Well, that's a change of tune, I must say!' Patty exclaimed. 'Good for you, Debbie! I'm beginning to think that this Manzù man has more to him than a palace! Have you fallen in love with him?'

Deborah stood stock still in the middle of the pavement. 'He's got a fiancée. She lives in a palace too.'

Even Patty was reduced to silence by this. It was left to Jerry to ask, 'Is he in love with her, do you think?'

'How should I know?' Deborah protested. But she did know. She knew that Domenico would marry Alessandra because she was suitable and because it was expected of him, but if it hadn't been for her father and his determination to reduce her relationship with Domenico to a matter of cold cash, she could have made him admit that it was *she* he loved, even if it were Alessandra he meant to marry. Only now she would never know for certain. He was proud enough, heaven knew, but she had her pride too and it had revolted at the prospect of being dangled in front of his nose on a golden string that would be operated by her father entirely in the interests of Beaumont International!

The apartment was small, too small for one couple to live in in comfort, let alone five people. Deborah tried

165

to make herself as small as possible, but whatever she did she seemed to be in somebody's way.

'I'm not surprised Michael's left,' she said.

'But I didn't!'

It was hard to tell who was the most shocked to see Michael's unkempt figure in the doorway.

'But——' Deborah made an anguished sound.

'I only went because you weren't here,' Michael went on smoothly. 'Now that you're back, I'm back too!'

The others groaned, but Deborah only stared at him. 'I'm sorry, Michael, but I didn't come back for you. It wouldn't work——'

'You'll never do anything without me!' he retorted.

'But I have to try.'

'If that isn't just like a woman,' he declared in disgust. 'You'll never be a sculptor, love! But you might have helped me to get somewhere! Your money would cushion my talent over the rougher places and we'd both have got something out of it!'

'My money?' Deborah said blankly.

'Beaumont's. Beaumont International's! Did you think we didn't know who your father is?'

Deborah went on staring at him as though she had never seen him before. 'No, I knew you'd met my father. He gave you five hundred pounds.'

'Yes, well'—Michael had the grace to look ashamed—'he doesn't want an artist for a daughter any more than I want one for a wife. Women ought to know better than to compete with their menfolk. They never have any real talent of their own.'

Deborah turned her back on him. Was it her imagination, or had the others moved closer to her, making a protective ring around her?

166

'I don't think there's any room for you here, Michael,' she said.

He took a step towards her. 'Is that your last word?'

Her eyes met his over her shoulder and she wondered what she had ever seen in him. He had no meaning for her now. He was only the shadow of a man and she was ashamed she had ever thought him better than he was. It came to her in a flash that when she had last seen him and listened to his opinions she had been a child. But she had grown up now. Domenico had seen to that.

'I'm sorry,' she said. 'Please go.'

'Okay, I'm going! I'm disappointed in you, Deborah. How did your father talk you into losing your soul? I hope you find his world big enough for you?'

'It has nothing to do with my father!'

'Of course it has!' he sneered with open contempt, and turned on his heel, leaving as suddenly as he had arrived.

Deborah sat down on the floor where she stood. 'I didn't think he'd go,' she said slowly, feeling like a pricked balloon.

'You know,' Mary told her, 'I think that the last few days have done you good! You'd never have told him where he got off before!'

'I'd never really seen him before,' Deborah admitted. 'Is it still raining? I think I'll take myself off for a walk —I want to be alone for a while. Do you mind?'

'So long as you're not running after Michael Doyle,' Mary said frankly. 'We'll expect you back when we see you, shall we?'

Deborah hurried down the stairs, wishing her knees felt better able to support her. She seemed to know all the things she didn't want and wasn't going to do, but what was she going to do with herself?

She looked up at the windows and saw her friends' faces peering out at her, and she was grateful for their concern. It was just possible that Michael could have been waiting down below for her. She wished the possibility had not occurred to her. She looked up and down the road with increasing nervousness, but he was nowhere to be seen. She took a step outside into the street and nearly jumped out of her skin as a quite different hand grasped her by the wrist and Domenico's angry voice exploded about her ears.

'*You* are coming with me!' he announced. 'Where have you been all afternoon? Your father——'

She presented a white and strained face. 'Has he been talking to you?'

'Not exactly,' Domenico reassured her. 'All I wanted to know was where you'd gone! Then I remembered you had the address of this place, and I turned your room upside down looking for it. But *what are you doing here*?'

She stiffened her back, hoping to do the same to her courage. 'I told you I'd rejoin my friends if I could!'

'So you did!' His expression changed to one of complete mockery. 'Funny, I thought you'd grown out of having to hide yourself behind their presence here in Rome. You told me many, many things, *spiache mia*, and not always in words. But now you are going to tell me something else—and you're going to tell me the truth!'

'I can't leave my friends!' she exclaimed, scared of what he was going to ask her.

'Then bring them with you!' he retorted.

She heard them then, pounding down the stairs behind her, and she thought she couldn't bear their curiosity about Domenico just then, no matter how kindly it was meant.

'If I come with you——' she began.

'Oh, you're coming!' He was so certain that she would allow herself to be dragged down the road after him that her jaw dropped. She'd show him she was not the spineless being he imagined! If necessary, she'd shout and scream and kick! But she did none of these things.

'Please, Domenico,' she said.

'Then you'd better come willingly,' he advised her. 'Because you're coming, if I have to carry you every inch of the way you're coming!'

Deborah's spirits failed her. Her friends spilled out on to the street behind her. 'What's going on?' they demanded.

Domenico bowed politely to them. 'Are you coming too?' he inquired. 'Deborah and I have a long-standing engagement for the rest of today. We were going to choose a piece of marble for her to work on, but it's too late for that now.' He studied Deborah's flushed face and her eyes widened with fright as she wondered what he was going to do. 'We are going to visit the Bocca della Verità instead. You see, I have something to ask her and I want to make absolutely sure that when she answers me she is telling the truth!'

Deborah's mouth was dry. 'I won't go with you!' she whispered.

'*Afraid?*' he demanded.

'You can't make me——'

'Can't I?' The special tone in his voice was too much for her and she made a mad dash away from him, only to find he had her by the wrist. 'Shall I have to carry you after all?' he asked her.

169

She shook her head, quite unable to speak. She had an unworthy suspicion that he was enjoying himself, whereas she felt a perfect fool. How dared he insist that she should follow him down the road, not caring one bit about the interested glances they aroused in the passers-by? And a few paces behind followed her four friends, delighted by their first meeting with Domenico Manzù. A fine protection they had proved to be!

'You can't be sure I shall tell you the truth even with the help of the Mouth of Truth!' she exclaimed, pulling vainly against him.

His only answer was to increase his grip on her wrist and to pull her more firmly against him. She cast him a speaking look and saw that he was *smiling*! How could he do this to her?

When they reached the portico of St Mary in Cosmedin, she was breathless from the pace he had set.

'I never thought you'd use force against a woman!' she threw at him as he released her arm, giving her a push towards the ancient drain-cover with its mask-like face.

She put her hands behind her back, refusing to so much as look at it.

'You don't *understand*!' she said desperately.

'Oh yes, I do,' he claimed. 'I understand only too well. But this has nothing to do with your father, or Alessandra, or anyone else but the two of us, *amante mia*, and I mean to have an answer in front of witnesses so that there will be no going back on it——'

'*I won't answer!*'

He patted her cheek with gentle fingers. 'Of course you are going to answer,' he encouraged her. He took her unresisting hand and placed it in the mouth of the

170

marble mask. 'My dear little love, did you really think I would let you run away from me?'

'I won't be bought and sold! I won't answer! I won't!'

He stood behind her, so close that she could feel the warmth of his body through her thin clothes and the unfailing excitement that gripped her whenever he came near overcame the last of her reluctance to give way to him. His own hand joined hers at the mouth.

'I love you, Deborah Beaumont,' he said. 'Do you love me?'

She wriggled her fingers, but she knew she wasn't going to take her hand out of the Bocca della Verità. She didn't even resent it. It would be such a relief to put it into words. She shut her eyes and the warm pressure of his fingers on hers was bliss to her.

'I love you more than life itself,' she said.

CHAPTER ELEVEN

SHE opened her eyes, shocked by what she had said. 'But then I don't know what love is!' She wrested her hand free of his and the Mouth of Truth. 'It doesn't make any difference anyway, does it?'

Domenico said something in Italian that she couldn't translate and took her bodily into his arms. He was surprisingly gentle. 'It makes this much difference,' he said, 'if you love me you're going to marry me!'

Her panic was plain to everyone present. 'I can't

marry you!' she exclaimed. 'I can never marry you!'

He smiled deep into her eyes. 'Of course you're going to marry me,' he coaxed her. 'I've already sent for your mother and invited all your friends! If you don't marry me, I'll come to England and sit on your doorstep until you take pity on me——'

'Don't be ridiculous!' she scoffed. 'Willow wouldn't suit you!'

The illusion was lost on him, but the implication was not. 'That is uncivil of you,' he rebuked her. 'Be insolent if you like, but never uncivil! That is the mistake your father makes in his handling of you——'

'Do you think you can do any better?' she demanded.

'Of course,' he murmured. 'I know I can do better!'

He certainly practised what he preached, she thought, for that was insolent enough. Yet she hadn't the heart to make an issue of it. She could imagine nothing more pleasant than to be handled by him—and he would be the one to call the tune between them, there was no doubt in her mind about that!

She sighed. 'I'll stay with you if you like,' she said aloud, 'but I won't marry you! I won't have it said my father sold me to you to gain a better deal for Beaumont International in Italy. Why, he's even discussed it with *your mother*!'

Domenico actually laughed. 'I doubt she understood what he was talking about,' he reassured her. '*She* had a far more interesting piece of information to impart to me, *piccina*! Something I wonder you didn't think fit to tell me yourself!'

She put her hand over his, opening his fingers one by one until she could stand away from him. So intent was she on what she was doing that she missed the tightening of his mouth as he watched her until he gave her a little shake to make her look up.

'I have been very patient with you,' he warned her, 'and not only because you are destined to be the latest item in the Manzù collection, but you will marry me just the same, *cara*, whatever foolish ideas your father has sown in your beautiful head. And do you know why you will marry me?' She shook her head, fascinated by the way his mouth moved when he talked. 'You will marry me because that is the only way I can be happy. You would not have me unhappy, would you?'

'Alessandra——'

'I forbid you to mention her name again! Alessandra will fulfil her ambition of giving herself to God and will be much happier than she ever could be with me. Whereas you, my little prisoner, will give yourself to me!'

'Will I?' Her voice trembled a little. 'Oh, Domenico, you can't want to marry me! We talked about it before and we decided against it——'

'When did we talk about it?' he demanded.

'Before,' she repeated. 'You explained about how you would have to leave me behind when you went to the Vatican——'

'Because I thought you were a Protestant like your father, but you are not, are you? Or so my mother tells me! Why didn't you tell me that? Did you think it would be of no interest to me?'

'I didn't know. I thought it was because I'm *me*!'

'Why should that make any difference?'

She found it hard to look him in the eyes. 'You have a name and traditions. Your mother——'

'My mother,' he cut her off, 'was worried at first that you were the product of a broken marriage, but only because she was afraid it might have fashioned your attitude to being married yourself. She asked many questions about your mother and you told her enough for her to know that your mother had never considered marrying again as your father had. She took it upon herself to ask your father why this was so. It was he who told her she was a Catholic, and it seemed likely, if your mother is Catholic so are you!'

Deborah pursed up her lips. 'That doesn't make me any more suitable as a wife for you!' she declared.

'No,' he agreed with a promptness that nettled her, 'but you have to admit it has its conveniences. There will be no arguments as to how the children are brought up, and the only reason I had for delaying the date of our wedding has now been removed. I would not have wished you to marry a Catholic knowing nothing of our faith, but now I can marry you with a clear conscience! You know all the drawbacks already and we have nothing else to wait for!'

'But, Domenico——' She felt quite breathless at the possibility he held out before her. 'Domenico, don't say any more unless you mean it!'

His hands were very gentle. 'You have your witnesses all about you,' he told her. 'We both know you'll marry me in the end. Won't you tell me so now?'

With a full heart she gave him the victory. 'Yes, please, I'll marry you,' she said, and she reached up and kissed him on the lips. 'I'll even accept my father's dowry if you say I must——'

'Certainly not! You bring me the talents of your hands and the gift of yourself, what more could I want, *carissima*? You may safely leave your father to me. He and I understand one another very well. I have already told him it is you I am marrying and not your family——'

'He wouldn't like that! Did he say he'd stay for the wedding?' She made a face at her own thoughts. 'Has he asked Agnes to come along?'

'We were agreed that Agnes would be decidedly *de trop* in the next few days. She has nothing to do with you!'

Deborah looked at him with awed respect. 'And you told Father so?'

'I did not have to,' Domenico replied, bending the truth without a moment's hesitation. 'Your mother will be arriving tomorrow and you are not to worry about her either. They will manage very well together, and so shall we. They are here as your parents. and as your parents they will be welcome. but our wedding day will be your day and for once they will both have to play second fiddle to you. This is your wedding. my love, and nobody is going to take it away from you.' He smiled and the light in his eyes made her gasp. 'Make the most of it, *mia moglie*, for afterwards you will be my prisoner for life, and what is mine I keep!'

Her lips trembled into a smile. 'I know that!' she dared to tease him a little. Hadn't he said before, *I saw you, I wanted you, and I took you. Isn't that enough for you?* And she had loved him then and longed for it to be true, and now it was. 'That's all I want too,' she said.

He cupped her face in his hand. 'I never thought you'd admit it,' he said. 'Was it so difficult?'

She wanted to tell him that there had never been any doubt about her feelings for him. that it wasn't that at all, but that she still didn't know what to do about her father and the use he would try to make of her as soon as she was Domenico's wife. Somehow she was going to have to prevent that, and she hadn't the first idea as to how she was going to do it.

Mary came forward and kissed Deborah warmly on the cheek. 'Good for you!' she congratulated her. 'And now that that's all settled, are you coming home with us?'

Deborah met her laughing eyes bravely. 'I'm going with Domenico,' she said, and she didn't mind their knowing laughter one bit. 'He may be a bully,' she added, 'but I like him——'

'Like him!' Mary exclaimed. 'You're head over heels in love with him!'

Deborah smiled a secret smile and put her hand back into the Mouth of Truth. 'Yes, I love him,' she said, and she buried her face in his neck, joining in his gentle laughter at her expense. 'Do you love me?' she asked, spreading her hand along his arm.

By way of answer he put his hand into the Mouth above hers. 'Yes, I love you, *ragazza mia*. Do you believe me now?'

She nodded her head, the colour storming up her cheeks. 'But I have loved you longer,' she confessed with a shy dignity that delighted him. 'I loved you from that very first evening. I knew I would never escape you then——even if I never saw you again.'

'What happened?' Mary inquired, much interested.

Deborah found herself laughing. 'He kissed me,' she said, and wondered a little that that was all it amounted to. 'I fell into his arms trying to get out of the bedroom window—and he kissed me!'

'Hmm,' said Mary, 'it sounds to me as though you were asking for trouble! You'd better go with him now before he changes his mind!' And she gathered up her

176

John with a loving look and led Patty and Jerry firmly out of the church. 'Don't forget to let us know when the wedding is!' she added over her shoulder to Domenico. 'We shall all want to be there!'

'I shall tell you myself,' he promised.

'Good.' Mary smiled and winked at him. 'Perhaps Patty and I will get to kiss the groom?'

'Why not?' Domenico indulged her, his eyes on Deborah. 'It will be my pleasure.'

'And Deborah's?' Patty put in dryly.

Deborah threaded her fingers through Domenico's. 'Why not?' she shrugged. 'I shall have John and Jerry to kiss me, won't I?'

Domenico's fingers tightened on hers. 'Make the most of it, *cara*, for after that you will owe all your kisses to me!'

'A jealous husband,' Patty remarked with disapproval, 'is always the worst kind.'

But Deborah only laughed. It wasn't Domenico's jealousy she was afraid of, in fact she found it rather reassuring that he should guard her so closely. She had no fears on that score, for she would be as proud of his ancient name as ever he could be. No, she was frightened that the one thing he would not be able to forgive was anybody else making use of that name for their own purposes. Alessandra would be justified in her worst fears that Deborah could only bring disgrace to Domenico in the eyes of his friends.

When her friends had gone, she turned towards him, her eyes dark with emotion. 'Domenico, my father——'

'Hush, my love,' he answered her. 'Your father is your father and there is nothing more to be said about him. Don't you trust me to look after you?'

Of course she trusted *him*! It wasn't that at all! But

177

how did one begin to explain that it was one's own father one didn't trust? And she didn't trust him at all!

'You don't understand!' she sighed. 'I suppose he has to stay in Rome for the wedding?'

Domenico frowned, his mouth settling into a stubborn line. 'He is your father and our guest, *cara*, and you will treat him as such.' His expression softened as he looked at her. 'He will not be here for ever, *piccina*! Come, it's time we were going home to relieve, my mother's mind that I have you safely back in my care! Parents have the right to worry about their children's happiness, though sometimes one might wish they would do it more quietly! My mother is very fond of you and she was in tears when she thought you were gone. I think she knows you hold my heart in your hands and would wish you to be careful of it! Shall we go and reassure her?'

Deborah said nothing, but she followed him out of the portico of the church and back into the street, her hand held close in his. It seemed to matter not at all to Domenico that it was raining again and that they would be drenched before they had gone a few yards.

'You should have brought an umbrella with you,' she smiled up at him, putting her worries firmly behind her.

'I should have done, but I had other things on my mind!' he retorted. 'If I have you back what can a little rain do to me?'

'It can ruin your clothes,' she reproved him. 'And mine too!'

She shied away from the look in his eyes, her heart thumping against her ribs. She was shocked by the speed of her reaction to him and how little control she had over her own emotions. It was worse still when he looked her over, enjoying the way the downpour had made her dress cling to her shape.

'I can always buy you more,' he suggested, sounding positively brazen to her embarrassed ears. 'Many, many more, for you to walk in the rain by my side and make muddy when I woo you in the Forum!'

She was breathless and tried to pretend to herself it was the pace he had set. 'It would be better if I learned to look after the clothes I have,' she said primly.

He grinned at her, suddenly young and carefree. 'Better for whom?' he teased her.

Mrs Beaumont fitted into life at the palace like a hand into a well-worn glove. She and Signora Manzù might have known each other for years, so closely did they agree about all the essentials of life. Deborah was proud of her.

'I wish Father would relax more,' she said to her mother. 'He's like a cat on hot bricks.'

'You're not much better yourself,' her mother said frankly. 'You are sure you're doing the right thing in marrying Domenico, aren't you?'

Deborah hoped she looked less desperate than she felt. 'I can't *not* marry him! But——'

'Yes? But?'

'I wish I had more to offer him!' Deborah burst out.

'And your father a little less?' Mrs Beaumont suggested with more shrewdness than her daughter had known she possessed. 'I shouldn't worry about it, dear. At the moment he has enough to think about because I have been made so welcome here and he suspects— thought he'd die sooner than admit it!—that Agnes would be rather less welcome. Poor love, he can't

179

understand it!' And she giggled like a young girl. 'I wonder if he was always so pompous?'

'Always!' Deborah said with feeling.

Her mother looked amused. 'Try to like him a little bit, darling,' she urged. 'You've always been as prickly as a hedgehog where he's concerned and, when he thinks about it, he's rather fond of his eldest daughter.'

'Mother! He doesn't care a row of pins about me! All he wants is to use me to further his own ends! If he'd been fond of me he would have taken some interest in my final show at the art college. *You* did!'

'But I might have gone along anyway,' her mother told her. 'Your father has never willingly looked at a statue or an original picture in his life!'

This time it was Deborah who laughed. 'Nor has Agnes! I'm sure she thinks it's slightly disreputable to be involved in anything artistic——'

'Ah yes, Agnes,' Mrs Beaumont said on a harder note. 'The immaculate Agnes with never a hair out of place.' She shook herself. 'How glad I am not to be her!'

'Heaven forbid!' Deborah agreed irreverently.

'Yes, well, she's nothing to us. And, talking about that last show of yours, I brought one of your pieces with me. I thought you might like to give it to Domenico. Of course, I didn't know then you were planning to do a bust of him. What do you think, dear?'

She opened her suitcase and rummaged about inside it, bringing out a small abstract shape that Deborah had done in her last year at the school. Deborah took it from her, balancing it on her hand. It had been carved out of a piece of wood and, with one's eyes half shut, it could have been a person standing, waiting, or it could have been an outsize wave breaking on the shore, or it could have been a tree bent by the wind but determined to survive.

'It's one of the best things I've done. But I gave it to you, Mother. I can't take it back now.'

Her mother fielded the carving neatly from her daughter. 'Then *I* shall give it to him! I've always liked it better than anything else you've ever done.'

She was as good as her word, choosing the dinner table as a suitable venue to present her gift to her future son-in-law.

'Deborah was too shy to give it to you herself,' she mocked her daughter gently. 'She's rather overawed by your collection.' She put the carving carefully into Domenico's hands. 'If you look,' she told him, 'you can find out quite a lot about Deborah from her work. And this piece is the most like her of any work she's done.'

'I can't see it's like her,' Mr Beaumont objected. 'Just a piece of wood, isn't it?'

Domenico ignored him. 'Has she always been afraid of losing her inmost self to outside pressures?' he asked Mrs Beaumont.

'I'm not!' Deborah denied hotly.

Domenico waved the carving under her nose, smiling. 'Where shall we put it?' he asked her. 'Next to the Michelangelo?'

Deborah's horrified reaction made them all laugh, all that is except her father, who stared at the carving with distaste, his face reddening. 'Do you mean you think it's good?' he jerked out.

'Good? One day Deborah Manzù will be mentioned in the same breath as Henry Moore or Barbara Hepworth. I shall certainly do everything in my power to nurture her talent. The children she will have to bear herself, but I can well afford nurses for them and keep most of the other domestic worries away from her when she's working. I shall be very proud of my clever wife! And who better to be her patron than her husband and the custodian of the Manzù collection?'

Mr Beaumont found this hard to accept. 'It will make a pleasant hobby for her,' he said with difficulty. 'But I can't help thinking that if she wants to work, she'd do better with Beaumont's. As a matter of fact, I've been thinking of expanding our interests in Italy, once all that unpleasant publicity has blown over, as it will do if it's given nothing else to feed on——'

Both the Beaumont women froze. Deborah cast Domenico an agonised glance and was shocked to see his face crease into an amused, even an indulgent smile.

'Can you imagine Deborah coping with any business venture?' he chuckled. 'It would take you a year to unravel the muddle she'd make of the simplest transaction!'

Mrs Beaumont's clear laugh rang out. 'How right he is!' she agreed. 'I'm sorry, but she's my daughter too! Don't you remember what a mess I used to make of the simplest household accounts?'

'If you'd paid it the least attention you'd have managed it on your head!' Mr Beaumont retorted. 'The trouble was you wouldn't *listen*——'

'It bored me,' Mrs Beaumont said simply without any visible sign of regret. 'Business is boring. Don't you agree, *signora*?' she turned to her hostess.

'Absolutely,' Signora Manzù smiled back.

Deborah caught the conspiratorial look that passed between the two women and her eyes met Domenico's in silent inquiry. Was it possible they had all known what her father intended and that they didn't *mind*? Indeed, far from resenting his plans, they were all thoroughly enjoying themselves in presenting a united front, as though they belonged together. None of them, not even her mother, was in the least afraid that her father would get his own way!

'Didn't I tell you not to worry?' Domenico murmured under cover of the general conversation that had followed Signora Manzù's *coup de grâce*.

Deborah picked up her knife and fork, her feathers decidedly ruffled that she should have been excluded from the conspiracy. 'As a matter of fact,' she said, 'I'm very good at figures!'

'Then you will be able to keep the family accounts,' he returned promptly. 'You will find them more to your taste than Beaumont's.'

But Deborah was not yet ready to make any such admission. 'How did you know that I didn't want to work with my father?' she asked.

Domenico shrugged. 'It would have been all the same if you had, you have other things to do. My wife may be a sculptor of renown, but she will still be my wife and she will have time for very little else besides!'

'Because you say so?' she asked, her eyes flashing.

'Because I say so,' he answered quietly. 'If you have any objection to that, I suggest you make it after dinner when we are alone.' He put out his hand and picked up the carving Mrs Beaumont had given him again. 'How right your mother is!' he exclaimed. 'Did you do this piece as a self-portrait?'

'Certainly not!' she denied.

'No? It is like you, nevertheless. But you, my darling, will never have to stand alone again, like this lonely little spirit. Isn't that worth ceding a little of your independence for?'

She tried whipping up her anger against him, but her

183

heart wasn't in it. 'I'll tell you that, too, afterwards,' she said.

But afterwards, just when she wanted to be at her coolest and most sophisticated, she was nervous to the point of stupidity.

'I shall put your carving in my study,' Domenico decided, running his fingers over the grain of the wood. 'Then I will only have to look up to see a part of you on my desk.'

Deborah flushed. 'Do you really like it?'

He looked at her in silence, his gaze sweeping over her face. He put a hand out to her and slowly, almost defiantly, she put her own into it, palm downwards, trying not to notice the tremble in her fingers as they touched his skin.

'You don't have to say you like it, unless you really do, just because I did it!' she blurted out. 'My mother should never have given it to you!'

His fingers closed round hers and he pulled her into the circle of his arms. 'Shall we take it into my study now?' he said in her ear.

She wanted to go with him badly, but she couldn't bring herself to admit it. 'What will the others think?' she put him off.

'That we want to be alone. Or don't you want to be alone with me?'

For two pins she would have denied it, but her natural honesty wouldn't allow her to pretend to him. 'You know I want that!' she said.

'I was beginning to wonder. What's wrong, Deborah?'

She held her head high as she preceded him through

184

the study door. 'Nothing is wrong. Why should anything be wrong?'

He put his head on one side and looked at her. 'You tell me,' he invited her.

She went over to the desk, watching in silence as he placed the carving where he could see it both from the leather chair where he read in comfort and when he was seated at the desk. She didn't want to tell him because she was afraid he would laugh at her and, somehow, that would be the last straw.

'I wanted to defend you from my father!' she burst out.

'And instead we stole your thunder and defended you from him?' he said. 'Was that so bad?'

'Not really,' she admitted. 'Only I thought I wouldn't be able to marry you because of him, and I thought I was the only one to see the difficulty, but you'd arranged the whole thing without me! Even Mother, who's always done everything he's asked of her, spiked his guns as though she'd been doing it all her life. She didn't look afraid of him once—it was as if he had no power over her at all!'

'My dear silly Deborah, are you afraid of him?'

She nodded, her eyes dark with remembered incidents from the past. 'He's very persistent——'

'But you're a Manzù now, and now that that has been explained to him he'll see for himself he has no hold over you, and as you were the only hold he had over your mother, no further hold over her either. He is your father, no more than that. Don't build him up into a bogey to frighten yourself with or I shall begin to think you don't trust me to look after you in every way. Cheer up, sweetheart, your father will know how to treat the future Signora Manzù with the respect that is due to her name and talent. You may believe me about that!'

It felt as though it was a physical weight that had rolled off her shoulders and vanished, leaving only a happy glow behind it.

'Oh, Domenico, I do love you!' she exclaimed.

He hugged her to him. 'That's much better,' he commended her, and then, 'I'm very glad to hear it, *spiace mia*, and now, could you hold your head so, and put your arms up so, and allow me to make love to you at last?'

'Oh, yes, *please*!' she said.

In the last six months Deborah had almost become accustomed to being Domenico's wife. Any fear she might have had that she would not be accepted by Roman society had long ago disappeared. Completely sure of her husband's love for her, she had achieved a new confidence and elegance that could seldom be ruffled nowadays by anyone but Domenico, who took a mischievous delight in changing his wife's cool public face to one of passionate response to his lovemaking.

They had made his study very much their own, perhaps the more so because they had to share the other public rooms in the palace with Domenico's mother and other relations whenever they came to Rome. It was into this room that Deborah came now, seating herself on the arm of Domenico's chair.

'It's finished!' she announced.

'Good,' he smiled at her. 'Does that mean I can bask in your undivided attention for a few weeks?'

She lowered her eyelids. 'For a few weeks,' she said.

He looked suspiciously up at her. 'What are you planning now?' he asked, amused.

'Another addition to the Manzù collection,' she murmured. 'At least, I think so.' She bent her head and kissed his cheek. 'I'll let you know when I'm quite, quite sure, but I'm too excited to keep it to myself until then. Are you pleased?'

He pulled her down on to his knee. 'You know I am! But it may interfere with your work, *cara*. Have you thought of that?'

'It will be work of another kind—and it will be for you! I'm glad I've finished the bust first, though. I promised you that right from the beginning. But this will be nicer still because it will be a part of both of us.' She wriggled free of his restraining hands and stood up, laughing down at him. 'Come and see the bust, darling. I meant it to be a very objective portrait, but I'm afraid anyone with half an eye could see that the sculptor is very much in love with you!'

He went with her at once, his hand on her shoulder as though he couldn't bear to be completely out of contact with her. Her old bedroom had been turned into a studio for her and the marble bust was standing on the bench, no longer covered by the sheet that had covered it for the past few weeks whenever Deborah was not working on it.

'What do you think?' she asked, eyeing it critically from the doorway.

Domenico was silent for a long moment. Deborah could feel his excitement as though it was her own, and was satisfied.

'Is that really how you see me?' he asked at last.

Looking at the strong lines chiselled out of the marble that were so like his own, she thought she had idealised him less than many another artist would have done. And it was a good portrait, revealing so

187

much about him that she had come to know and love.

'It's better than the wood-carving my mother gave you,' she said dispassionately. 'It's the best thing I've ever done.'

'Yes, it is,' he agreed. 'The other was done by a child, but this was done by a woman. You're a greater artist than even I had thought. It would be a shame if you were to neglect such a talent.'

She leaned against him, her happiness full to overflowing. 'But I want to have babies too,' she told him. 'There's more than enough time for both!'

He kissed her. 'And?' he prompted her.

She turned towards him, glad to give him his answer. 'And best of all is being your wife! I would give up both art and motherhood if they meant I couldn't be the Signora Domenico Manzù! But aren't I lucky that I don't have to?'

His hands became more demanding against her body as he smiled deep into her eyes, seeking the passionate response he knew he could arouse at will.

'May you always think so!' he said against her lips.

She buried her fingers in his hair and drew his head down, congratulating herself that the glint of purpose in his eyes meant that he had no intention of going back to his study alone.

'Do you think your mother will excuse us for dinner?' she murmured.

A quiver of laughter answered her. 'She is thinking of inviting your mother to keep her company,' he told her, 'she sees so little of us!'

Deborah made an inviting sound of satisfaction and lifted her face to his. 'What a good idea!' she said. 'They can both get used to the idea of being grandmothers to our son together! *Domenico——!*'

188

But her protest went unheeded. 'Then come to bed, woman, and stop nattering!' He opened the door, hurrying her out of the makeshift studio. 'Besides,' he said, 'how do you know it'll be a son? If she's like her mother, I think I'd like a daughter!'

Deborah sighed, trying to look downtrodden and succeeding only in looking flushed and eager. 'If you go on like this we shall end up with half a dozen of each!' she rebuked him, her eyes heavy with passion.

He pulled her into his arms and kissed her warmly. 'And whose fault is that, my darling?' he retorted. But she was no longer listening, happy once again to be a prisoner in his arms.

Harlequin
understands
Love...

and the way
you feel about it...

**That's why women
all over the world read**

Harlequin
Romances

Beautiful novels with that special blend
of Harlequin magic...the thrill
of exotic places, the appeal of warmly
human characters, the tenderness
and sparkle of first love.

Enjoy six brand-new novels every month —
contemporary romances about women
like you...for women like you!

Available at your favorite bookstore or through
Harlequin Reader Service

In the U.S.A.
1440 South Priest Drive
Tempe
AZ 85281

In Canada
649 Ontario Street
Stratford, Ontario
N5A 6W2

FREE Harlequin romance catalogue

A complete listing of all the titles currently available.